MURDER AND MISCONCEPTION

A BEN TIME MYSTERY

T.A. HUGGINS

NEW YORK

NASHVILLE • MELBOURNE • VANCOUVER

MURDER AND MISCONCEPTION

© 2018 T.A. Huggins

All rights reserved. No portion of this book may be reproduced, stored in a retrieval system, or transmitted in any form or by any means—electronic, mechanical, photocopy, recording, scanning, or other,—except for brief quotations in critical reviews or articles, without the prior written permission of the publisher.

Published in New York, New York, by Morgan James Publishing. Morgan James is a trademark of Morgan James, LLC.
www.MorganJamesPublishing.com

The Morgan James Speakers Group can bring authors to your live event. For more information or to book an event visit The Morgan James Speakers Group at www.TheMorganJamesSpeakersGroup.com.

Publisher's Note: This novel is a work of fiction. Names, characters, places, and incidents are either products of the author's imagination or used fictitiously. All characters are fictional, and any similarity to people living or dead is purely coincidental.

ISBN 978-1-68350-510-5 paperback
ISBN 978-1-68350-511-2 eBook
Library of Congress Control Number: 2017904788

Cover & Interior Design by:
Megan Whitney
Creative Ninja Designs
megan@creativeninjadesigns.com

In an effort to support local communities, raise awareness and funds, Morgan James Publishing donates a percentage of all book sales for the life of each book to Habitat for Humanity Peninsula and Greater Williamsburg.

Get involved today! Visit
www.MorganJamesBuilds.com

CONTENTS

ACKNOWLEDGMENTS

I would like to acknowledge my husband, who dutifully read and reread the entire manuscript for railroad technicalities. He put in his nearly forty years of railroad service only to retire and become my faithful proofreader. Thank you, dear, for your love, expertise, and help. I would also like to thank my editor, Katherine, for her work, suggestions, and kind words of encouragement. Morgan James Publishing; my Acquisitions Editor, Terry Whalin; Angie Kiesling, the Fiction Publisher; and Gayle West, Author Relations Manager; were also invaluable with their suggestions and encouragement as we moved the manuscript to the final product. Finally, I want to always include a hallelujah for my Savior and Lord, who guides and directs my path.

PREFACE

As the wife of a railroader I have heard many accounts of incidents that have occurred on many a train trip. I have changed to some degree the facts so as not to embarrass, incriminate, or undermine those involved (mainly my husband). However, I have tried to be true to the work-a-day life involved in modern railroad employment. This is a fictional work. Characters, names, and incidents are products of my imagination and not to be thought of as real. Any resemblances to actual events, organizations, or persons, living or dead, is coincidental.

CHAPTER ONE

SAINT LOUIS,
NOV. 6, 0130 EST

I awoke with a start, the phone blaring in the night. I hadn't set an alarm in twenty-some years. The phone took its place. I rolled over and picked up the handheld unit, then mumbled out my "Hello." The automated female voice replied with the familiar "Railroad calling," and continued with the menu options. I punched in my employee number and a series of numeric choices in the dark. Practice makes perfect. A real live female responded, "Mr. Time, you are on the E103 at 0130 hours."

"Who is my conductor?"

"Mr. Evans," she said, followed by a click and the dial tone. I really don't need to ask who the conductor is for my return trips. I do this because, when startled awake, I am uncertain whether it is a return trip.

After the phone call, I have two hours to make it to the railyard and be ready to move the 1:30 AM train. I have therefore trained my body to lie in a semi-coma for about a half hour and then to move into a vertical stance and wander into the nearest shower. The shower usually brings me into consciousness.

I dressed in jeans and a flannel shirt, placed my toothbrush back into my grip, and was ready to descend to the hotel lobby.

The night man, Steve, was reading his iPad.

"Hey Steve. How's it going? Have you seen Evans yet?"

"No, have some coffee. I just made it, and there are some cookies left."

"I think I will," I mumbled. I poured some black magic into the Styrofoam cup and added two packs of sugar.

"Hope the coffee does the trick tonight, and hope Evans is on time. He's got the reputation of oversleeping, and we're on duty at 1:30 AM."

I took several small sips of Steve's stiff brew. "Looks like our van is coming a bit early. Do you mind ringing Evans' room?"

The sound of the opening elevator door caused us to turn in that direction. It revealed Evans standing under the lone transom light. Like Lurch from *The Addams Family*, he declared, "You rang?"

Evans stands six feet seven. He has a broad forehead and speaks in a baritone voice, slowly and methodically. Most trainmen call him, appropriately, "Lurch." On the railroad, we rarely use a man's given name. My mother named me Benjamin James Time. The trainmen call me Big Ben. I prefer to think it has nothing to do with my protruding stomach, but rather because you can set your watch by my actions.

"Come on, Lurch. We need to board our limo. The railroad waits for no man or beast. I'm the man. You're the beast."

"Why did we get called so early?" Evans mumbled. "We were four times out [fourth on a list to be called out for a train] when we got in yesterday. I thought I'd get at least six hours of shuteye."

"I don't know, but I haven't had eight solid hours of rest in two weeks," I replied.

As I slid the van door open I said, "Hi Chuck. You on night duty?"

Chuck, the driver, nodded and said, "Yep, and a cold night it is. Do you guys want to stop by Subway for some eats?"

"We sure do," I responded.

Lurch, just beginning to awaken, said, "I think I'm going to diet and skip the sandwich."

"It's a twelve-hour trip home. Are you sure? You will be crying and complaining like a little schoolgirl, begging for some of my sandwich before we even get to Casey."

"I need to lose a few. Got a new honey on the line."

"You need to do more than just lose a few," I called out as I left the van. I ordered an Italian sandwich for Chuck as well as my favorite ham and cheese. While I watched the assembly of my sandwiches, I thought about the reason Chuck took up driving the rail limos, which are truly just minivans. Chuck retired some five years ago from a maintenance job. A couple of years back, his wife got cancer. After they had to declare bankruptcy, Chuck started driving the vans to chauffeur train crews around day and night. They barely scrape by, but his wife needs one last round of chemo. I returned to the limo and handed Chuck his sandwich.

"Thanks, Big Ben. I appreciate the kindness and the supper."

We made small talk as we proceeded to the yard office. I glanced back at Lurch and saw that he was peering intently at his cell phone—probably the new honey.

The yard was relatively small, located just east of Saint Louis. The gray-brick yard office was an unwelcoming dreary sight in the middle of the night. Nevertheless, it was the portal to home. As Lurch and I entered the office, we heard the familiar voice of Indiana, fellow engineer, short and loud, shouting, "That should be our train. We've been waiting for two hours!"

The trainmaster bellowed back, "I assign the trains. Yours will be along any minute."

"You said that two hours ago," Indiana replied as he stomped off, giving us the stink-eye.

Lurch walked stiffly past Indiana and grabbed our bulletins off the printer. He turned and approached the yardmaster, Jesse, one of the few females able to withstand this male-dominated culture, for the work order. We were in luck and received both sets of documents, a rarity in this yard office. We hurried out of the office while the getting was good. The trainmaster could have given us Indiana's late train. That would have meant at least five more hours here while we built that train in the yard. It was a great relief to have escaped the onerous task of train building.

As we made our rapid retreat I heard the trainmaster once again shouting at the train dispatcher, "I can't move all those trains. They won't take the blasted things in Indianapolis." He added some colorful language to make his point. George the Tyrant, master of the trains, ran the show and wanted all of us lowly trainmen to know it.

We left the office and made a beeline to the van, which took us to the train. This train was just passing through, my favorite kind, a run-through. This was also my lazy conductor's favorite kind. As we approached the engine we could feel the vibration of the ground beneath our feet. It was a rhythmic movement, a familiar movement, a comforting feeling in a dark night. Lurch picked up my grip with his and lifted his long legs onto the platform. I was thankful for his help. My legs were half as long as his and my belly twice as wide. I could barely reach the first step without my grip. With thirty pounds of accessories in hand, well, I had been described as a troll heaving a bag of rocks up a four-foot ledge. As I pulled my body up, I thought that maybe I should have skipped the sub sandwich, but I would never let Lurch know.

I walked through all three engines making sure they were all online, all switches turned on, the engines ready to move, and hand-brakes released on each one. It looked like good power tonight. I loved the newer units, the wide bodies with that new-car smell, but I would never tell the guys, because it was manlier to complain. I returned to the seat and provided Lurch with three-step protection, speaking this phrase out on the radio. Three-step consists of: automatic brake fully applied, generator field breaker down, and independent brake fully applied. It protects the conductor from train movement while he walks back and releases hand-brakes on all cars that are tied down. Lurch removed the hand-brakes and called on the radio, "You can release my three-step, Fatboy."

I responded, "Three-step is released, and I'm pumping it up. Get your lazy butt back up here so we can head for home."

While awaiting his return, I did my air test. Sure glad the EOT (End-of-Train Device) was working. The EOT takes the place of cabooses and five-man crews. We no longer have enough men running a train for a good card game. I slowly wiped down the handles with Lysol wipes. I have learned it helps keep the flu season at bay. If we miss two days a month, we can be fired. It makes getting through flu season difficult. Everyone works, sick or not, which does not further our cause of staying healthy.

This engine had come from the West Coast. We would move it to the middle of the country, to Indianapolis, home for us. Another crew or two would shepherd it to the East Coast. As I pulled the throttle out, I saw the lights of the railyard begin to dim, and finally they were swallowed up by darkness.

I always love the rising whine of the engine as we increase our speed. After we reach our target speed of 60 miles per hour, we can relax for a while and enjoy the passing scenery.

Lurch rearranged himself in his chair. I could tell he wanted to talk. Sure enough, he started rambling on about his new honey, name of Kim. "She is tall, blonde, blue-eyed, and loves me." He seemed to be quite smitten.

I asked, "What are your plans concerning Kim?"

He responded, "Dinner and a movie." Then he laughed at his own joke.

I sat quietly, thinking he was not ready to discuss this subject yet.

After some time and several calls of "clear signal" (a conductor's mandatory signal calling), Lurch announced that he might ask Kim to live with him, since his work prohibited them from spending much time together. He continued, "She doesn't care for the late-night calls, the daylight sleep, and the 'I can't go to the mall. I'm one-time out' stuff. Lately, with being called out on my rest, I haven't been seeing her at all. If she lived with me, well, at least I could see her for an hour or so before sleep or before the next trip."

I heard his argument. I understood his argument. My own wife gets tired of an absentee husband. I haven't had a holiday off in fifteen years. We don't get weekends off. We don't get any scheduled time off other than vacations. I am on call morning, noon, and night. She hasn't been able to say, "Yes, my husband and I will attend," to any invitation in fifteen years, and this is hard for her. I've seen her cry just twice over my lack of schedule. Both times it made me momentarily hate my job.

I asked Lurch, "Do you love Kim?"

He just nodded in the affirmative.

"Do you think you will stay with the railroad?"

He responded, "Of course. Where else can I make this kind of money?"

"Well, then, Kim will have to get used to this lifestyle. Give her time. Living together, however, is not God's will. Getting married is God's will and His blessing to man. Do you believe this?"

"You're the chaplain of the union; I knew you would say this or something similar, and I don't agree. That's old-fashioned thinking."

"Well, as chaplain of the union, I have to speak up," I continued. "Do you know the definition of fornication? Would you make Kim a fornicator? Or do you love her enough to make her your wife? Think about this. Talk to her about what she can expect from your schedule or lack thereof. I would hate to see you go the way of Indiana . . . four wives, five children with different mothers, multiple child support payments that he is still paying.

He has torn apart four different families, his children, his wives, grandparents, aunts, uncles—all lives affected and all lives brought into suffering. All these lives in chaos. You've heard his complaints, his tirades. I bet all three of the states we run through have heard Indiana complain."

"That makes my point," Lurch said. "He married them all. He may have kept himself from some of the chaos had he just lived with them. Would have saved himself some money too."

"No, it would have just left five kids wondering who their father was and why he left, would have made four women and himself sinners against God and themselves—would have just left even more chaos and suffering in his wake. God makes rules to save us from ourselves to make life cleaner, better, simpler, to form godly men, women, and children, families . . . society. Think about it, Lurch."

Lurch responded, "Approach signal ahead."

I repeated, obeying the rule, "Approach signal, I'm getting hold of this train." Approach signals indicate that an engineer should sit up and take notice. Miss one, and it may cost a life.

The night gave way to dawn, and home loomed on the horizon. We had passed Effingham. I gave Lurch half my sub with hope that he was still speaking to me and that I could lose a few pounds just for the effort.

Between bites I said, "Hope the main is open when we get there so we don't have to yard this beast." I heard Indiana's voice on the radio. He and his crew of one, the Mad Russian, were just starting out from St. Louis. They would be furious! I didn't blame them. They were just beginning their trip, eight hours after their call.

Lurch responded with a head nod. At least he was still awake.

Three hours later I saw the clear signal.

"We're going down the main, Lurch."

I kept the throttle off in idle as we headed down the main, ready for this trip to be behind us.

Upon arrival at our home base, Lurch grabbed his grip and headed for the yard office. I was left to wait for the outbound crew to take the train. While waiting, I packed my grip. When I saw the next crew, I made the big step to dismount the train. After nodding to several passing trainmen, I heaved my grip into my truck and headed home. This wasn't a bad trip, on duty eight hours and forty-three minutes. I wished they were all that fast. I called my wife and warned her of my approach.

"Hey Myrtle, you want to go out for breakfast and stop by that auction this morning?"

She responded, "Sure, how close are you?"

"I will be there in fifteen minutes, so get rid of your boyfriend. Ha-ha!" I laughed at my own joke.

"I'll be ready, and I'll kick Renaldo out the door," she responded.

"Don't toy with me, you saucy wench," I stated with my best Ricardo Montalban accent.

She responded, "What rerun is that line from?"

"*The Dick Van Dyke Show.*"

"See you when you get here. Love you."

She loved auctions, and I loved breakfast. It was a win-win all around.

Two hours into the auction I felt ready to collapse. The auctioneer's voice was lulling me into a stupor. When my head started to bob, my wife asked, "Do you want to go home? There's nothing I can't live without today."

"Lead me home, Myrtle." I call her Myrtle. This is not her given name. Her given name is Debrah Sue formerly Cane, now Time. She has studied long and hard and now is officially Dr. Time.

She tells her students, "Call me Dr. Deb." We've been married for some thirty years, and we dated seven years before we married. We met when she was fifteen. According to her parents I robbed the cradle. We have two daughters. The younger is married, and much to everyone's surprise I love our son-in-law. I don't feel outnumbered by women when he is around. Our oldest is single and lives in Oklahoma. We do not see her as much as we would like to. We are now empty nesters, and my wife reminds me that this affects her much more than it affects me.

When we arrived home, she sent me off to bed and went on with her mysterious life. Or so I imagine. *What does she do with all her time?* I wondered as I nodded off.

I felt her shaking my arm. "Ben, Ben, wake up. It's the railroad calling."

I couldn't quite come out of it and shook my head like a wet dog, a groggy wet dog, and took the handset.

"Hello," I mumbled.

"Mr. Time, you have the W369 at 2100."

"Who is my conductor?" I asked.

The male voice responded, "Evans."

I heard the click and thought, *Here we go again*.

I hated this train, and so did all the others. We stop and pick up cars in Effingham, get pulled into sidings often to let the van trains pass by or any other old freight train that is out there. Then we put the power away in St. Louis. It generally takes all twelve hours and more. We call it the "Bone Crusher."

Still confused despite the shower, I left the house with several sandwiches of homemade meatloaf Myrtle had made in hopes we could have dinner together. But not tonight, not again. I wondered if Lurch would be speaking to me tonight. Maybe the half-sub made some inroad.

At the yard, I heard the normal complaints. Crews had waited hours at Cadillac Road, just outside the yard, and in Illinois there was a signal giving a false positive and turned from clear to stop without an approach signal. The final complaint was that Indiana came in threatening everyone in his path. He was still hot over his long delay.

Lurch deftly retrieved our paperwork, and we were off again. Seemed like we were never released from duty.

Our train left on time. A good start, once again in the

black of night. For a long time we were silent, except for the normal obligatory railroad speak.

Eventually Lurch said, "The Mad Russian was Indiana's conductor. He told Old Joe that Indiana was ready to pummel George the Tyrant at the yard. The Mad Russian had to hold him back. He said he was sick and tired of George himself, but was getting more sick and tired of trying to keep Indiana cool. Said he would like to let Indiana go ahead and pummel George, but that he would get pulled out of service with Indiana if Indiana did his dirty work and pummeled George. The Russian said that he couldn't afford to get pulled out of service. It seems the guys are getting short on self-control."

I replied, "It's been this way before, too much work, too little rest, and egos that are too big. Someone will probably get pulled out of service. That decreases the number of available workers and increases stress from lack of rest. Tempers just get hotter. Not a good cycle. George pushes the wrong buttons and continues until he breaks someone. He has done it before. Right now it's Indiana's turn."

Lurch sighed. "I hope he doesn't turn on me. Don't know what I would do."

I just nodded and continued to peer into the black night as we got ready to pull into the first siding for the evening.

Ten hours later we were sitting at the signal ready to yard our train in St. Louis. We had the signal, but we needed permission to enter the yard. We called the yardmaster several times, but nobody answered. I gave a clear warning into the radio that we would soon be dead, outlaw, because we were getting close to the twelve-hour time limit set by the government. Usually that warning got our train moving, but not today. Just silence.

Lurch asked, "Wonder what's going on? Usually George would be yelling at us by now."

"I know. Well, I guess we just sit and wait. I think I will get some sleep, I'm exhausted," I replied.

We both closed our eyes. We woke abruptly when we heard pounding on the engine door. They had sent a van for us. I checked my watch. It had been twelve hours and fifty-three minutes on duty. I was surprised we slept without radio interruption.

"Hi Betty," I half mumbled. "What's going on?"

Betty, today's limo driver, was seventy-three years old. Puffing on a cigarette, she leaned against the door of her van. "I have no idea. I was ordered to come and pick you guys up, and two other drivers were ordered to go get two other crews. We'll find out soon enough." She stubbed out her cigarette on a nearby tree and got into the van.

Lurch and I were both foggy and attempted to make sense out of being placed in a van without further radio talk on the train. We discussed this new development with few words. Soon we spotted the railyard in the distance. As we got closer, we spotted flashing lights. Slowing as we approached, we could see a firetruck, ambulance, and two police cars. Lurch and I got out of the van much more quickly than we climbed in and entered the yard office. I spotted Jonesy and Ty.

"Hey! What's going on?" I asked.

Ty responded, "Looks like they found George the Tyrant dead by a switch in the yard."

"Do they know what happened?"

Ty shook his head. "Haven't heard."

Hearing footfalls, I turned to see Jesse, the yardmaster, running from the back of the building toward the front. Several more officials seemed to be arriving. I thought they must be railroad suits. One of them shouted at us to clear the way. At that moment, a stretcher with a body narrowly passed us in the hallway. We four all stood smashed against the dingy wall and looked at one another, quite unsure what to say or do. Several firemen and EMTs passed by us as if we were all invisible.

Finally, Lurch looked at me and asked if he should go to the computer and finish up our time slips and paperwork. With lack of expertise in such a circumstance, I just shrugged. Jonesy and Ty seemed equally unsure of their next move.

Two more crewmen walked in. It was obvious that dispatchers were still dispatching trains. It was becoming a real circus, but no one was in the ringmaster's seat. I still felt quite dazed. This all seemed to be one big, very bad dream. Finished with our paperwork, Lurch punched my shoulder and mumbled, "Let's go to the van."

I followed him with a bad feeling in the pit of my stomach—not sure if it was from lack of rest, the homemade meatloaf, or the sight of the body on the stretcher, covered with a white sheet.

Once inside the van we told Betty what we knew. She replied in her gruff, cigarette-smoking voice, "I know a brakeman who was killed by a switch about fifteen years back . . ."

Her story seemed to descend into the muted trumpet sound on the Charlie Brown cartoons, "Wha Wha Wha," as I began to nod off once again. At the hotel, Lurch and I got our room assignments and headed our separate ways. Maybe I could make more sense of this event after some sleep.

CHAPTER TWO

SAINT LOUIS,
NOV. 8, 1030 EST

The next morning I awoke with the memory of the stretcher covered in white, and remembered that George the Tyrant was no longer here on this planet, no longer with us. I wondered about his family. I believed that he was divorced, but not entirely sure. I wondered if he had children. How old were they? I wondered if George had any relationship with the Lord. He was here one day, seemingly determined to make our lives miserable, and gone the next. I thought of my own mortality, and I spent some time in prayer with the Lord.

The ringing phone interrupted as usual. I answered, "Big Ben here."

Surprisingly, it was not the automated "Railroad calling." It was Lurch. "Hey, Big Ben, come downstairs. We have a table for six for breakfast."

I hurried and showered, packed my grip, just in case we were called out soon, and descended in the elevator.

I spotted the guys—Lurch, Jonesy, Ty, the Mad Russian, and Indiana—all deep in conversation in the far corner of the dining room. As I approached the table I realized that the topic for the morning gripe session would not be the usual.

"Hi guys!" I greeted everyone.

Somebody replied, "Hi Ben." This response was unusual. I usually got "Hi Fat Boy," or "Hi Big Ben and getting bigger," or other similar remarks.

I ordered coffee and Eggs Benedict and joined the conversation. "I am surprised to see you guys here. Did they cancel your train?" I asked Jonesy.

"We waited at the yard office for three additional hours, watched the railroad suits move back and forth without a word, and watched Jesse get interrogated, but we couldn't hear a thing they were saying. They finally sent us back to the hotel. We heard that trains were backed up all the way to Effingham. They were trying to get Tim, the second trick trainmaster, to come in when we left. Chuck brought us back to the hotel."

Indiana said they were deadheaded, brought the whole way here by van rather than train. He and the Mad Russian just checked into the hotel. Indiana added, with a loud voice, that George got what he deserved and that was all he was going to say about the whole business. The Mad Russian just sat there looking sullen. Maybe he was exhausted, or maybe he was just living up to his name.

Lurch asked if anyone knew how the accident happened. Ty thought he had heard one of the EMTs say there was blunt force trauma to the head.

"Why do you think George was out at that switch anyway?" I asked.

Indiana, not keeping his word to be silent on the subject, jumped in. "He was probably setting the switch up for a test to create a failure—to pull a crew out of service. You know he was like that. Always trying to set us up to pull us out of service."

"Well, he might have been checking car numbers on the adjacent track," I responded.

Jonesy said, "I heard that a crew had a hazardous material car that wasn't on their train consist [order of cars on the train] but was located within the six leading cars. A big failure. So George was probably out checking the train consist."

Indiana piped up again, "Yeah. George was probably ready to pull the conductor of that crew out of service for that one."

Lurch said he had reported to the yardmaster that there was too much tension on the switch one month previous. He nearly received a jaw kick on that rainy night from the old Mason-Dixon switch. He added that maybe some other crew reported the switch as well. George may simply have been checking the switch.

"Well, maybe Jesse, the yardmaster, can shed some light on the accident. She was there."

Suddenly, the familiar ringtone "Don't Worry Be Happy" sounded, and all the guys realized that I was getting my call to go to work.

I answered, "Roger, 1030 for re-crew and deadhead home. I'll let Evans know. He's here with me."

Lurch leaped up from the table. "Wow! We're in the money this trip!" Shouts of "Two trip tickets!" —better known as a "double dip call"—came from all around the table.

Chuck picked up Lurch and me at the hotel and took us to the yard office. Chuck was seemingly aware of George's death since he had been shuffling crews around most of the morning. The whole yard was a tangle of yesterday's delays and bad news. Bad news travels faster than the trains.

"You two pulling in a train from the east side of the yard?" he asked.

I nodded and asked how his wife, Shirley, was doing.

He responded, "She is not handling this new chemo well. Sick most of the time. But the doctor said she might go into remission once the treatments are done. I hope so. It has been rough."

"You guys are in my prayers, Chuck," I replied as Lurch and I left the van and headed into the office for our paperwork.

The yard office was quiet, eerily so. Lurch looked at me with a confused frown, shrugged, and headed for the printer. I shook my head and walked to Jesse's office to offer my condolences. I knocked and found that she was not on duty. Leo was holding down the fort, and he was busy.

Without further contact, Lurch and I left the building trying not to disturb the silence. We climbed back into the limo with Chuck and headed for the train, the W211 that never made it in yesterday. We relieved the exhausted crew almost as silently as we left the yard office. This was a strange day. We made our preparations to move the W211 in. Thankfully, it didn't take long. The dispatchers were anxious to get things moving again.

Lurch dismounted and strolled into the yard office. I lagged behind, then dismounted. Curiosity usually gets the best of me, and questions were whirling in my head around that switch that supposedly killed George. It wasn't far to the culprit, the Mason-Dixon switch, so I moseyed over to take a look. The same switch that Lurch reported last month. Too much tension can make the armature swing up when you release the switch stand keeper. Excessive tension can break the conductor's jaw or even kill him. I decided to check the switch myself. First I moved the switch from right to left then from left to right. The Mason-Dixon seemed to have the proper tension. However, if it were not working properly when George was out here . . . well, they would have fixed it by today.

When I entered the yard office I spotted Andre, another yardmaster. He nodded when he saw me and said, "Hey Ben. I guess you weren't expecting to see me. I was supposed to be off for two weeks but got called in for today. Apparently Jesse got very upset over the George thing and asked off. She seems to get about any time off she wants. Must be nice being female." Andre seemed absorbed by papers he was aimlessly shuffling, as I saw Lurch coming in behind me.

"Have you heard anything more about what happened to George the Ty . . . I mean George?" Lurch chewed his lip.

"Well, they said the switch arm came up and hit him right in the temple and killed him dead. The railroad suit said that they looked over the switch, and it had excessive tension on the switch stand lever. When George put his foot on the dog [switch stand keeper], the switch stand lever sprang, and the switch stand lever ball caught him on the right temple. Jesse found him dead near the Mason-Dixon."

"That switch has been reported by more than one crew. What a nightmare! What a way to go," replied Lurch.

Lurch was probably thinking that it could have been him lying there dead yesterday.

I was pondering that we really don't know the length of our days. That line of thinking was taking me nowhere, so I frowned and said, "Lurch, let's head for home."

CHAPTER THREE

SAINT LOUIS,
NOV. 8, 1800 EST

We climbed in the van with Chuck and soon were both snoring. This often happened when we were being deadheaded. Our bodies know when to get caught up on sleep, which is any time they get the chance.

It seemed that only moments had passed when we were awakened as the van bounced over the Indianapolis tracks. Chuck must have noticed our movements in his rearview mirror.

"We're home again, boys. You've got your second ticket, second pay for the trip. Wish I got that benefit," he said. "Apparently you both have caught up on your beauty sleep. Although more sleep probably couldn't hurt if you really want to be beautiful." He chuckled to himself.

We began to come back to life, grabbed our grips, and headed for the Indianapolis yard office. While the paperwork was being done, I called my wife to let her know I was back. She didn't answer. I was not even sure what day it was. That's the thing about having no schedule. Days, nights, how many days have passed? It's all a blur. Then I remembered it was Monday evening—church board meeting night. Deb always took the minutes. She wouldn't be home until nine o'clock or after.

It was lonely walking into an empty house—no kids, no dog, no wife. Once home I opened the refrigerator just out of habit, a bad one, and looked for the makings of a meal. I wasn't sure which meal to search for—breakfast, lunch, or supper—but I felt pretty sure I had missed one. There in the left corner was a container of meatloaf. Meatloaf sandwiches again. I made a plate and sat down to watch a little TV. I had had some rest, and I began to think about George. I had not reclined long when my cell rang.

"Ben," Indiana hollered into the phone. As I held the phone further from my ear, I thought my wife was correct—all trainmen are hard of hearing, and they all yell into their phones.

"It's me," said the voice.

"What do you need, Indiana?" I responded, not at all happy to hear his loud voice.

"The cinder dick has called me into the yard office to interrogate me. He's asking all kinds of questions: Where was I at the time of death? What was I doing? Why was I mad at George the Tyrant? Et cetera! I told him I hated the son of . . . Oops, I won't say that to the chaplain. Anyway, I told him why. I asked him why he was asking me all these questions when George got himself hammered by the Mason-Dixon switch? And he just said he was fact-finding. I don't like being interrogated, Ben. What does it mean? I was off that day, at home. You know that."

"Indiana, maybe he was just fact-finding like he said. I'll call a friend in the railroad police department and ask a few questions. You know the railroad has its own police and claims departments that investigate all accidents on property."

"I knew that I could count on you. A brother in the same union and a chaplain to boot. Thanks, Ben." Click. Dial tone.

What a change of tune. Indiana usually hated me for my chaplain views. His life was one of continuous chaos—womanizing, gambling, and drinking whenever possible. He was loud, selfish, and obnoxious. However, I did wonder why they were questioning him, when it appeared that George's death was accidental. So I dialed John, my friend in the railroad police department, a cinder dick.

"Hi John. This is Ben Time. It's been a while since I've run into you. How's it going in the policing business?"

"Same as usual, the usual thefts in the yards, and we had one switch accident. It was lethal. I bet you're glad you're no longer a conductor, Ben."

"Yeah, for a lot of reasons. I know about George. The St. Louis dicks are questioning a fellow engineer, making him nervous. Do you know why?"

"Well, Henderson, in St. Louis, is trying to make a name for himself. He lives railroad and is a railroad buff to boot. It seems he was looking at some old switch accident photos, and George's photo doesn't show the same type of injury markings as the old photos. He's also into conspiracy theory stuff. He is probably just trying to move up the ladder. Tell your friend it will pass as soon as Henderson gets it out of his system."

"Thanks, John. I will pass it on. Stay safe." I texted the summary of the conversation to Indiana then went back to watching *NCIS*. After a half hour of *NCIS* I thought, *No wonder some guys are conspiracy theorists. They watch too much TV.*

Soon I heard Deb call out, "You made it back! Just got back from church. Didn't expect you this soon."

"We got deadheaded home. I slept the whole way and didn't call to remind you to get rid of your boyfriend."

She gave me a kiss on the top of my balding head and told me about her evening. "It was a long meeting tonight, so it will be a long typing session tomorrow."

Then I told her about our trip. She asked me several of the same questions that I asked myself the morning following George's death: Was he married? Did he have children? How old were they? Was he a Christian? I told her I didn't know the answers to any of those questions. She said I wasn't as personable as I should be or I would know these things. She may be right, but I wouldn't admit it. I told her that she really doesn't understand the relationships between management and union employees much. She said she would pray for George's family and added, "Ben, I've got to get some sleep. It's 10 PM, a little past my bedtime."

"Well, I slept the whole trip back. I can't sleep yet, so I'll watch some real man TV." I started changing the channel before she was out of the room. Just then my phone whistled informing me I had a text. *Probably Indiana*, I thought as I pushed in the code. To my surprise, it was a text from the Mad Russian.

"Call me when you get the chance. MR."

I was not up to another phone call just then, so I phased out and watched three episodes of *The Virginian*.

CHAPTER FOUR

INDIANAPOLIS, NOV. 9, 1300 EST

woke up to the phone ringing once again. This time my call was for the W333 for 1300 hours with the Mad Russian. Some trainmen boards marry the conductor with the engineer. Both respond to the same call at all times. Our board does not. The conductors follow a rotation, and the engineers follow separate rotations. So we never know who we will be working with. I worked with Evans two trips in a row. This trip was with MR, the Mad Russian. *Oh well*, I thought, *working with him saves me a phone call*. I'd talk with him at work. I walked through the house searching for my wife, who apparently was not home. I found a note on the table. "Marcia and I went garage sale-ing. Should be home about 12:30. We can do lunch. Love Deb".

I know she expected me to be home longer, but once again I disappointed her. I had to be at the yard by 1300 hours. I left before she arrived home. When I arrived at the yard office, I saw MR getting the paperwork ready, so I started toward the engine. Day and night in the Indianapolis yard, the ground vibrated, the smell of diesel fuel permeated everything, and retarders squealed their high pitch of metal-on-metal sound that can be heard for miles. I threw my grip up and then heaved myself up. I began my routine to get the engines ready to move west. The Mad Russian's grip thudding on the floor startled me. He didn't follow it, so I assumed he was walking the train. I had my own "moving out" work to do. I finished as the Russian settled into his seat beside me.

He said, "Sure am glad you're my engineer this trip. I have had it with Indiana. Had three trips in a row with him. I think other conductors move down on the board if they think he will be their engineer. I can't afford to do that, but if this was going to be another trip with that short, freaking loudmouth, I would have just had to lose the trip. I'm done with him."

"Is that why you texted last night? Were you just needing to blow off steam?" I asked.

"No. Indiana called me and screamed on and on about the questions he was asked concerning George's death. He said I would be interrogated when we get to St. Louis tonight. I wanted to ask you if I should have a union rep with me and why they would be interrogating us anyway if George was smacked by the Mason-Dixon. Aren't they just harassing us?"

I explained to MR just what I explained to Indiana about Henderson, the overzealous cinder dick assigned to the case. There would also be a claims department investigation with perhaps even more questions.

"We have to comply with railroad investigations, so just hang in there," I added.

MR got quiet except for calling out the signals. I was glad for the quiet as we passed the empty cornfields and leafless trees. I saw two deer in the fields eating stubble and was glad they weren't on the tracks. I have hit more deer than I care to think about.

I knew MR was going through a divorce and had two children, so I decided to stay away from asking about his wife, but I thought I'd ask about his kids.

"They're doing okay considering. Jeff played Pee-wee football this fall and did a good job. Ana isn't doing very well in school. I had a parent-teacher conference two weeks ago. She is becoming very withdrawn and failing two subjects. Now that their mother is living with a drug addict, I'm keeping them, but it takes a lot of family help. When I call down on the board to take some time off, it has to be for them. I can't afford to call down or off just because I am working with a lunatic like Indiana. I just don't need the extra stress that he brings."

"I admire you for sticking with your kids through all this, Russian," I replied.

We stopped to get several additional cars and then continued our trip. This trip was going pretty smoothly.

Yet darkness always seemed to fall so suddenly in November. The rest of the trip would be in the black of night. Trips do seem longer when they cross from day to night or night to day.

I had bought an Arby's chicken salad sandwich for the trip. I started eating, and so did the Russian. We continued eating and talking. The dispatcher had us pull off into another siding. It was a cold sparkling clear night in November. We don't get too many nights in November in which the sky is brilliantly lit with stars. I decided to walk out onto the catwalk and stood admiring the night sky, one of my favorite things to do when I'm set out on rural sidings. I was surrounded by the remnant of corn, and the heavens were decorated with pinpoints of light, more than I could ever count. A few moments on the catwalk reminded me of God's sovereignty over his creation. Soon the peaceful moment ended with radio chatter, and I realized it was time to bring the horses in.

When we neared the yard, we were immediately given permission to move the train in.

The Russian broke the silence. "They are probably moving us in so they can interrogate me. Can you stick around, Ben?" he asked.

"I'll wait, but I have no authority to come into the room with you. Just tell the truth, and don't be concerned. I don't think this will amount to anything."

We took the ponies to the barn and dismounted. The Russian was lagging behind tonight. I glanced back and saw him stop and stare long and hard at the Mason-Dixon switch. I walked into the office hoping I could speak with Jesse and get her to talk about George's death. She still wasn't back. Andre was working.

"Hi Andre, how's it going tonight?" I asked.

Andre replied, "Same ol' same ol', but with extra faces. The railroad dicks and claims people have both been poking around, and I'm still working for Jesse. It's all I can do to keep things moving. Got to go, Ben, the phone's ringing. Did the Russian go see Henderson? He's been waiting."

"Yes, I think so. He's been dreading this. I'll be sitting in the locker room killing time."

I sat down and looked over to see if there was any coffee in the pot. There was some, but I changed my mind about drinking a cup for fear I would stay up all night instead of sleeping. I decided to text my wife and see if she was awake. When she didn't respond, I assumed she was sleeping.

To pass the time I decided to text my daughter. Trish is a waitress and is often up after midnight. I got lucky. She was up, and we discussed her apartment decorations and her mother's opinion on painting a room purple. Deb didn't care for the idea, but Trish was going with her own decorating sense, or lack thereof, according to Deb. Facing the usual differences of opinions, I told my daughter I was ignorant on decorating matters, and she concurred. After several more rounds of texting I decided to roam.

I could see the back of the Russian's head and part of Henderson's face through the office window. Henderson noticed me at the door, so I quickly crept away. I wasn't sure what to do next, but it occurred to me that I should go back and look at the Mason-Dixon switch again. The yard is usually well lit at night. However, I noticed that there were two lights burnt out—one close by the switch and the other located at the west end of the yard. I stepped over the tracks and approached the switch. I moved it both left and right again. It worked correctly. I stopped and took a long look at the yard from the switch.

Just what was George doing out of his office? Was he looking to set up a crew for some failure? Was he testing the switch? I was drawing a blank and started to think back when I was a conductor. I could clearly remember when I had walked the tracks, counted cars, and pulled switches. Hated it when it was 17 degrees below zero and the winds were blowing. Miserable switches would freeze up. Glad I'm not a conductor any longer. I don't think this once-Herculean body of mine could take it now. I wouldn't dare admit this to any of my conductors, though. I continued wondering why George was out here. That question needed to be answered. I kept wishing that Jesse was back so she could shed some light on the matter. I looked the area over one last time and still hadn't a clue. I needed to find out if Henderson had interrogated Jesse yet and what he may have discovered.

I walked back into the yard office just as a door slammed. The Russian was leaving. He picked up his grip and stormed toward the exit. I walked to the locker room, picked up my grip, and followed the Russian's lead. Much to my surprise there was a van waiting for us. Looked like a new driver, at least a new face to me. The Russian slid into the front, so I threw my grip into the back seat and bent my chubby body into riding position. I could tell the Russian was in no mood to talk, so I turned my attention to the new face.

"Hi. I'm Big Ben, what's your name?"

He responded, "Jake." Suddenly, I was thrown back against the seat as Jake, the new face, accelerated from 0-50 miles per hour as if we were in a drag race. Still trying to sit upright, I thought, *Either this kid doesn't know the speed limit here, or he just doesn't care.* The acceleration seemed to mesh with the Russian's angry mood. I decided to sit back and hold on for dear life and leave conversation for another time.

I exhaled a dramatic sigh of relief as we pulled up to the hotel. In fact, the hotel never looked so good—a safe haven in the night. I dragged out my grip and walked toward the sliding glass doors. Once again, I was several steps behind the Russian.

As I entered, I greeted the night desk man. "Hey Steve."

Steve responded, "The Mad Russian is sure living up to his name tonight. What's up, a rough trip?"

"No, the hours are just getting to him, and our limo driver is training for the Indy 500. I think I'm pretty beat as well. See you in the morning after some beauty sleep."

Steve chuckled. "Hope it works for you, Ben."

I entered the elevator just as Ty was leaving. Ty said he was called for the E133 and was supposed to meet with Henderson as well. "What do you think that cinder dick wants with this black man?" he asked.

"He seems to be interviewing anyone who was in the yard office when the accident occurred. He just interviewed Indiana and the Russian. Were you and Jonesy there when the accident happened?"

"I'm not sure what time George was killed. We were there from 0400 until we saw you guys come in. Are they interviewing Jonesy as well?"

"I don't know. Probably."

"Well, Ben, I don't like being the only black man interviewed. Should I get the union rep?"

"No, just answer with the truth as you know it. I was told that Henderson is just trying to move up the ladder with his theories. See you later, Ty. I need some sleep."

"If I need some support, can I count on you, Ben?"

"Sure. Remember, Ty, we're brothers from a different mother." The elevator door slid shut.

CHAPTER FIVE

SAINT LOUIS, NOV. 10, 1200 EST

I awoke once again to the phone ringing. This time it was my cell, and it was blaring loudly. I must have slept through some of the rings. It is set to increase in volume with each successive ring, and it was getting loud. I answered and discovered I was being summoned to breakfast by the Mad Russian. I decided to meet him and find out what Henderson had asked the previous night. Maybe the Russian was ready to talk.

I finished up my morning routine quickly, packed the grip, and descended for nourishment. As I entered the restaurant I spotted the Russian's noticeably large frame sipping coffee in the booth in the right-hand corner of the room.

"Morning, Russian, how's the coffee?"

"Could be better, could be worse, Ben. A lot like my life."

I sat, and the waitress quickly brought my coffee and took my order. The staff recognized the railroaders and got us in and out rather efficiently. I appreciated them. Some of the guys acted like real jerks toward them. I looked over at the Russian and asked if he wanted to talk about the interrogation. He nodded, sipped, and listed the questions that he had been asked: What did you think of George? Was George fair with the trainmen? Was he fair with Indiana? What was Indiana's relationship with George? Did you feel the same about the man? How long did you wait for your train in the office that day? Did you get the following day off? What did you do that day? Did you ever have trouble with the Mason-Dixon switch? On and on Henderson had droned with questions.

I finally asked, "What were all the questions for? George got whacked with the switch. End of story."

The Russian frowned.

"Exactly. Why harass me? But he did tell me George's skull markings were not consistent with other switch accidents. He was there to make sure this was an accident, not a murder. Then he told me to stay marked up, so he could question me further if necessary. That really fried my bacon. I always work, I'm always marked up, and you know it, Ben, and you know why. I hate Indiana for getting us in this mess."

"When we get back I'll call my friend in the police department and see if Henderson is really a problem. Did

Henderson mention all the people he was going to talk with? Did he mention if he had talked with Jesse? I think we need to know why George was out there."

"He didn't tell me anything."

"Maybe Jesse will be back when we get our call. I know Henderson is interviewing Ty, and I think Jonesy as well, if that is any consolation."

His phone rang. "We got our call, Ben, the E465 at 1200. I am going back to the room and pack my grip."

I nodded and began devouring my Eggs Benedict.

When we entered the yard office a few minutes later, it wasn't as quiet as it had been. Things appeared to be getting back to normal. I decided to see if Jesse was in. It was good to see her right where she belonged.

"Hi Jesse, how's it going?"

"Don't ask, Ben. I came in, and the first thing I am greeted with is Henderson wanting to grill me, and grill me he did. It's hard enough to return to this trash hole.

"Has George's death been hard on you? Why was George out there at the Mason-Dixon switch?"

"Don't ask me. I have enough to do and keep track of. George is not in my job description. I've got to get back to work, Ben."

She turned and stalked off. I had been dismissed.

I trudged out to the train. I was disappointed that I had received no more information from Jesse. Clearly Henderson was raising the hackles of, well, just about everyone he spoke with. I decided that when I got home I would again call John, my friend in the police department. I would find out if he knew anything more about the investigation.

I was thoroughly ready to move toward home by the time we received permission to exit the yard.

It was one of those dreary days where the blandness of the sky matches the lifeless landscape. The Russian and I both seemed lost in thought, so at least half the trip went by in relative silence. There was some radio chatter, signal calling, and the hum of the engines. All of it white noise, a noise that can draw one back into sleep if not careful. Finally, the Russian said, "Ben, I wasn't totally honest with Henderson."

"About what?" I asked.

"Henderson asked me what I did with my time off the day after our very long trip home. I really didn't think it was his business, so I just said sleep and some housework."

"Well, what did you do that day?"

"The day before with Indiana was a long fifteen-hours-plus day. I did get about five hours of sleep when I returned home. Then I drove back to St. Louis. I've been seeing someone in St. Louis, and we had an argument. My mom had the kids, so I went back to straighten the matter out. I am trying to communicate better and not let this relationship end like my marriage. I stayed with her several hours and drove back. I didn't think this was any of Henderson's business. But if he finds out I was back in St. Louis, I may be in trouble."

"I wish you had told him the truth. Do I know the new gal?"

"Yes, but I prefer not to tell you who she is yet."

"I'll call John and see how the investigation is progressing. I'll let you know what I find out. Jesse was pretty mad about being interrogated. She didn't seem to know a thing about why George was outside that night. Ty is also upset about being interrogated, and Indiana is always upset period. I haven't run into Jonesy, but my guess is that he will be interrogated as well. I'll get back to you if I find out anything new, Russian."

"Thanks, Ben."

The chatter died down again. We both were lost in thought for the rest of the trip home.

CHAPTER SIX

INDIANAPOLIS, NOV. 10, RETURNED AT 0300 EST

This wasn't a bad trip. Once home I went straight to bed. My wife was actually at home and sawing some logs herself. I thought as I began to fade away, *Good thing I'm not a thief.*

I woke and glanced at the clock. It was 1100 hours. The other side of the bed was empty, and the room was blackened with the curtains pulled. I sat up and stretched. Everything hurt. Age has been letting me know it is slowly but surely causing my decay. I wandered out into the family room hollering, "Myrtle, are you around?"

She yelled down the steps, "I am upstairs typing. Be down in a minute. There are some pancakes and bacon in the microwave."

"Thanks." That was great news. I stumbled into the kitchen and hit one minute and thirty seconds on the microwave and waited for breakfast. I grabbed the plate, added my light syrup, and proceeded back into the family room for a well-deserved breakfast at home.

As I was finishing my plate while watching *Gunsmoke*, my wife came into the room.

"What time did you get home last night. I never heard a thing?"

"I noticed. I could be anyone coming in. You never stirred. I got home about 3 AM. Anything new around here?"

She said that our oldest, Trish, had fallen at work, hurt her knee, but really couldn't afford to be off. They didn't do a CAT scan because the immediate care there didn't have one, so she was home today with leg elevated and on ice. She added, "I hope it's okay." She paused, looking thoughtful.

"The Thompsons, at church, are going through a rough spell. Bob has been hospitalized with a hernia, and Jane is still going through radiation treatments. Their boys never come around anymore. I'm taking a meal over for dinner tonight, and I offered to do up their laundry while Jane is spending so much time at the hospital. The college called to see if I would consider teaching a course this winter semester. I do enjoy teaching part-time, but I declined because of the drive and winter weather. I'm done risking my life for work. I will continue with the education projects though. It may be cold and lonely here without you, but I hate winter driving. I think I'll start tutoring some here at home. What do you think?"

I replied, "Whatever you want to do is fine." I have learned through the years that this is the smartest response. "Do you think we should send Trish some money until she gets back on her feet?" I asked.

"I don't know, I'll call and feel her out tomorrow. I have to be tricky. She won't let me know right away if she is in need. I'll be a detective tomorrow."

"Speaking of detectives, I feel like one since George passed away. There is a railroad dick named Henderson. He thinks that George came to an untimely end through foul play. He is investigating and interviewing some of the guys. This is upsetting our fine rail ecosystem. Anyway, I have been trying to cool down hot tempers that are starting to become infernos."

"Why do the guys go to you? You aren't the union rep."

"Well, I am their union chaplain, which either infuriates them when they act like heathens, or if they feel threatened enough by our employer they seem to welcome my input. I'm no longer their biggest enemy. There are some questions about George's demise that I would like to see answered as well. I sure don't want to think someone did George in, especially someone I may know."

"Do you have some time at home today?" Deb asked.

"Yep, what's on the agenda?"

"I'd like to start some Christmas shopping. You want to come? We can have a bite out for lunch. Then when I get home, I'll cook for the Thompsons."

"Okay, I'll get showered and dressed, and we can be off."

I didn't love Christmas shopping, but I got so little time with Deb that I did what I could when I could. I knew too many railroaders with broken marriages not to give shopping a try.

When we got home, I carried in about a dozen plastic bags filled with "Christmas treasures."

I sat down and decided it was a good time to call John and see if he knew anything more about the investigation. Deb went to the kitchen to perform her culinary magic for the Thompsons.

Before I dialed, I wrote down several questions:

What specifically made Henderson think this was not a switch accident? What was George doing outside at the switch? Who is Henderson's leading suspect? Have the city police been called in or the NTSB (National Transportation Safety Board) or the FRA (Federal Railroad Association)? Has the railroad claims investigation been performed?

I looked up my contacts and found John's number. He answered on the fourth ring.

"Hey John, this is Ben. How's it going with our local gendarmes?"

"Okay. Well, Ben, since this is the second time I've heard from you in a week, I bet it's about the St. Louis so-called accident."

"You're right, John. Henderson's still interviewing and rattling everyone he interviews. I have a few questions, and I thought maybe you could answer them. Then I can pass on the answers and calm a few interviewees."

John answered my questions as best he could. I jotted down the answers. Then I sat silently thinking about his points. I was surprised to find out that the blunt trauma to George's head seemed to be at the wrong angle if indeed he stood at the switch properly. Another surprise? The switch was still in the switch stand keeper when the body was discovered. That fact made it appear that the switch had never been released. However, there was blood on the ball of the switch stand lever. John added, for my information, that most switch injuries are back injuries not head injuries. The police department thought this may be a murder because of the incorrect angle and the position of the switch still in its switch stand keeper.

I also learned that no one seemed to know why George was out at the switch. And Indiana was still the leading suspect. He had no alibi for his whereabouts that night, and he made the most noise about wanting to get even with George. The city police department was informed, and the railroad claims people were working on their reports. The FRA and NTSB were notified. Henderson was lead investigator. He was interviewing any crews that were in the yard office at the time of death. John didn't remember the names of the crew members that were there that night, but I knew it was Ty and Jonesy being interviewed. Indiana and the Russian were being interviewed and would most likely be interviewed again. Jesse, the yard master, was on duty that night, and she was a suspect as well. And finally,

Chuck, the limo driver, was being interviewed since he was waiting for a crew in the yard at the time of death. Henderson had convinced the captain of the railroad police department that the case was a murder case, and he was given permission to pursue the investigation.

I decided to put what I knew about the case in my phone under Notes. I listed all the interviewees, where they said they were between 0100 hours and 0500 hours, and what, if any, motive they may have had. At this point I really only had the Mad Russian, who said he was in St. Louis with some gal unknown to me. And a possible motive of some financial stress. I did add that two lights were out in the railyard, and one was near the Mason-Dixon switch. I needed to find out far more information about the rest of the gang being interviewed, considering it really was a murder case now.

I thought I'd give Lurch a call and let him know what I knew. He answered on the first ring, which surprised me. I gave him the rundown on what I had found out from John and asked if he had heard anything new in the last couple of days.

He said, "I've worked with Jonesy, and Jonesy was interviewed by Henderson as well. Jonesy didn't seem to be upset by his interview. He basically told Henderson that George had screwed him over on a few calls. This seemed par for the course for everyone who dealt with George. Jonesy also added that one of his conductors had complained about the tension on the Mason-Dixon about a month ago. He thought the problem was fixed because he hadn't heard any more complaints. He said he and Ty had been called for the E134 for 0300, and they were in the yard office at the proper time complaining that their paperwork wasn't there. Both Jesse and George seemed either to be in their offices or missing. They weren't within Ty and Jonesy's sight. So they sat around drinking coffee and griping."

Lurch continued. "They may have talked an hour or more and were getting impatient when they heard Jesse through her office door talking rapidly on the phone. They thought maybe something had happened in the yard, and that something was what was delaying them. Sometime soon after they heard Jesse talking, they heard sirens. At some point, they found themselves plastered against the wall while all kinds of people rushed through. I think, Ben, that's when we came in. I sure thought this whole thing was just another railroad accident, and I am very surprised they now believe it was murder."

I told Lurch that I was surprised as well. At that point I was two times out and had just enough time for a nap then the work call. He was three times out and planned some dinner with Kim and then maybe some shuteye, if time allowed. Much to my surprise, Lurch said he hoped the next trip would be with me. I guess he has forgiven me my mini-lecture on marriage.

In the kitchen I found that Deb had left to take dinner to the Thompsons. She left me a small casserole of baked spaghetti and meatballs to warm and eat at my desire. I fell asleep watching a rerun of *The Andy Griffith Show*. When

I awoke, I was wondering if Henderson was anything like Barney Fife. I called my stand number and discovered I was now first out. I decided to eat my spaghetti and meatballs and lie down to await my work call.

CHAPTER SEVEN

INDIANAPOLIS,
NOV. 11, 2100 EST

O nce again I was jolted awake by the phone. This time a real person's voice informed me that I was on the W133 at 2100 hours and with none other than my good friend Lurch. *Two good deals*, I thought while moving toward the shower. The trip was with Lurch, and I might be able to get some more shuteye while waiting on a siding later tonight.

Lurch was waiting for me at the railyard. I jabbed his shoulder.

"You sure are one lucky fellow to get me as your engineer for the night."

"It was either win the Publishers Clearing House Sweepstakes or get you as my engineer. I picked you."

"Thanks."

I hoisted myself up onto the engine. Lurch threw his grip up and began to walk the train. I focused on my own checklist for the trip. We were soon underway. It wasn't long before our conversation drifted toward the main topic ever since George's untimely demise—the murder investigation. I thought maybe Lurch had learned something new after our conversation about Jonesy.

"I hear Indiana's at the top of the list," he said, shaking his head as if he couldn't believe such a thing. "Henderson thinks Indiana isn't being straight with him about his whereabouts that night. I expect Indiana's waiting to be subpoenaed." He paused as if he were trying to find a better way to say what he knew to be true. "Indiana apparently told Henderson it was none of his bloody business, slammed the office door, and left. He sure knows how to win friends and influence people."

I told Lurch about the notes on my phone about each interviewee, thinking that when we got placed on a siding I would add his information to my notes. There wasn't much more to say. Lurch called a couple more signals.

Suddenly I thought I saw something on the track. Lurch must have thought the same, because he yelled, "Put it in emergency!"

I yelled back, "Too late, it won't help!"

Then, *blam!* A huge tree had fallen over the track. The train struck it at full speed. As the tree splintered, shards torpedoed against the engine window. From somewhere we heard a deafening blast. Both Lurch and I ducked in fear as I threw the train into emergency. A full-speed freight train does not stop on a dime. I was so afraid that it seemed to take forever, but we probably didn't go more than a mile before it finally came to a complete halt. We had to assess the damage. Because I put the train in emergency, Lurch had to walk the entire train. We radioed the dispatcher that we had stopped and why.

What a mess. The front window was cracked and windshield wipers were broke. There were gigantic splinters and debris all over the catwalk. There was damage to the right side of the engine. This had to have been one monster tree that we had just turned into kindling.

Lurch and I were mystified by one problem. The rails are designed to prevent exactly such an accident. An electric current runs through the rails at all times. A computer somewhere monitors that current. If an object touches both rails at the same time, the computer triggers a rail signal that should have alerted us to stop. We had just passed two "all clear" signals. We puzzled how this could have happened. It was hard to believe that either this tree had fallen at the unlucky moment immediately before the impact, or the tree hadn't touched both rails simultaneously.

After reporting the damage, we were given permission to proceed. I know it took at least an hour for my heart rate to return to normal, and I think it took longer for Lurch's heart rate to slow. He didn't speak for an hour and a half. I have operated an engine for more than twenty years, a lot longer than Lurch has been riding the rails. I've hit some doozies: a man trying to commit suicide, a truck devoid of passengers, a car with one passenger, multiple deer, a cow, and many much smaller animals. It is terrible to know you can't stop and may be taking a life or lives upon impact. It leaves a long-lasting void in the pit of the stomach. This was my first blast with a full-sized tree.

We continued in the blackness of night without incident. Somewhere past Effingham we were told to turn onto a siding. I pulled off and was still too hyped up to do the usual and drowse. So was Lurch. By this time we needed to talk about it. We speculated what force it took to turn a full-grown oak instantaneously into matchsticks. I told Lurch the trainmaster would probably come out to greet us to inspect the damage once we reached the yard. He would view the speed tapes as well. I wasn't worried about being pulled out of service because we were five miles an hour under speed. Lurch was happy to hear that because he could also be pulled out of service had I been violating the speed limit.

I took out a meatball sandwich and nibbled on it. Lurch pulled out a Reuben from Arby's. After a while I got my phone out to type some additional notes. I added Indiana as chief suspect and noted that his whereabouts at the time of George's death were still unknown, because he had been unwilling to say. In addition, I added that Ty and Jonesy were at the yard office in the break room waiting for their paperwork, and Jesse's whereabouts seemed to be unknown. I also added Chuck as being in the parking lot of the yard office. Lurch muttered that he was sure glad we didn't get to the yard office until after they found George. I agreed.

We were soon radioed to leave the siding and go on our way. Several hours later we got the word to proceed directly into the yard. This didn't surprise me, because the powers that be would be fuming over engine damage and hoping to pin it on our negligence. As we dismounted the engine, we were greeted by the trainmaster, Tim. He wasn't a bad sort, but he was management. He began to inspect the front engine and asked us to hang around.

It was a beautiful night, and as Lurch went into the office to finish up the paperwork, I decided that I would sit somewhere close by and watch the inspection. I wandered over some rails and found a tailgate down on an M&W truck (Maintenance of Way, the guys that keep the tracks in good order) at the west end of the yard. There seemed to be no M&W crew here, but the tailgate was down as if a crew were loading or unloading. This was unusual because Joe, the M&W man, was fastidious about his truck. I sat down on the tailgate and peered over at the Mason- Dixon switch, willing it to speak its secrets.

Still stiff from the trip, I found it hard to get comfortable. I readjusted my seating to watch for Tim as he inspected the engine. While shifting my position, I bumped into the end of a spike maul. I turned around to push it further back into the truck and noticed some muddy-colored debris on the end of the maul. Again, this was unusual for Joe, the obsessive-compulsive M&W man. I keep a tiny a flashlight on my keyring, and I took it out to look over the spike maul. It appeared to have dirt and some strange stain on the working end. I decided rather hurriedly that I would give up watching Tim do his inspection. Henderson might be in the office, even if it was the dead of night. For that matter, maybe Joe, the M&W guy, was in there as well, since his tailgate was down. I needed to investigate.

I grabbed my grip and walked toward the office, mulling the possibility that this dirty spike maul had anything to do with George's death. As I entered the door I saw Andre.

"Hey, is Joe around here tonight?"

Andre frowned. "No, he's been off all week on vacation. Besides, he certainly would not be around this time of the morning."

I told Andre Joe's truck tailgate was down, which seemed very unusual to me. I decided not to tell him about the spike maul. I walked around the corner and saw Henderson sitting in the extra office so I knocked. He looked up and said, "Come in."

I entered and introduced myself. "Mr. Henderson, I'm Ben Time, an engineer out of Indianapolis."

Before I could continue he replied, "I know. I know you are a friend of Indiana's as well. I may have some questions for you about that guy. Wait out in the other room. I'll call you when I'm ready."

As I backed out of the office, I saw Lurch with our papers in hand. I told him I had to wait for Henderson to summon me, so it might be a while before we could get the van to the hotel.

"What does Henderson want with you?" he asked. Then he mumbled, "Wonder if I'll be next."

Looking for a place to sit and rest, I thought it would be hard to predict what Henderson might want next.

Lurch fiddled with his papers. "Oh, is Tim back from inspecting the engine?" I was pretty sure that Tim was still inspecting and hinted that maybe he could go out and check on Tim. It wouldn't hurt to keep an eye on the progress of the inspection. Lurch went back out the door into the night.

I sat for some fifteen minutes before I heard my summons. I took the chair in front of the detective's desk thinking maybe if I answered some questions I could also get some answers to my questions.

Henderson was a short man, shorter than I. Also much thinner. He wore wire-rim glasses somewhat out of date. His dark eyes were also small, but intense. He had made me wait until he was ready. He seemed to move constantly. He stood while I sat, and he made it obvious he was forcing me to wait until he was ready to begin his interrogation. I recognized the signals of a man who insisted on control.

He began by telling me that he represented the railroad police department and was in charge of the murder case of George Berry. He continued, "I am currently interviewing all parties who were present in this office on the night of

George's death. I have asked you to come in to give me some insight into Indiana's personality. Indiana mentioned your name, and I am curious to know the relationship between the two of you. So, what is your relationship?"

"I'm a fellow engineer, in the same union, but that is basically it."

"Why would Indiana throw your name around during our interview?"

"I don't know, we certainly aren't close. Ask him."

Henderson paused his pacing. "Did George ever hold you out, away from home terminal, longer than you thought necessary?"

I could answer that one easily. "Yes, a good many times over the past fifteen years. George seemed to like to control people and ruffle feathers. I'm sure most of the guys will answer yes to that question."

"Do you think a man might kill over that, over being held away from home?"

"A man might murder for far less. It depends on the nature of the man." I noticed I had the attention of the man who insisted on being in charge. He had leaned against the wall.

It seemed like a good time to ask a few of my questions. "Mr. Henderson, have you discovered why George was out at the switch that night?"

He peered at me through his wire rims, making his beady eyes even smaller.

"I hear that while George and Jesse were talking that night, George said he thought he spotted the W123 pass through a switch through the yard. He told Jesse he was going out to check the switch's position, that maybe he would need to pull that crew out of service. But Mr. Time, I'm asking the questions. Were you present in the Indianapolis yard when Indiana returned from that trip?"

"No. I was not."

"Have you overheard at any time any other trainmen threatening George?"

"I have to think about that one. Conversations about management, especially those who enjoy pulling the guys out of service, are often threatening. Most of the conversations are just a way to relieve steam. Probably healthy in some way."

Henderson gave me a hostile glare and said, "You can go, Mr. Time. I may have some more questions later."

"I understand. Mr. Henderson," I replied, thinking that I could "Mr." with the best of them. "Is it true that you thought this case was not a switch accident because of the switch position and that the skull markings were not consistent with other switch accidents?"

"True but . . ."

I interrupted again. "Mr. Henderson, I was seated on the tailgate of Joe's M&W truck a half hour ago. Joe, the M&W guy, has not been around for a week. He never leaves anything out of place."

"So?" Henderson spat out, clearly perturbed by my continuing the conversation beyond his summons.

"So, as I was saying, I was trying to get comfortable in the truck and felt the working end of a spike maul in my flank. I looked it over. It was covered in mud and some weird stain. You may want to look it over yourself. It's hard to prove murder without a murder weapon since you are negating the switch as the culprit." Before I got the word *culprit* out of my mouth, Henderson was up and out the door.

I guess that ended our conversation. I walked out too and saw Lurch talking with Tim. They said goodbye, and Lurch and I walked out to the limo. It was early dawn. I liked this time of the morning, but I was feeling the weight of the past twenty-four hours. I asked Lurch, "Did Tim agree that we were not negligent in the engine damage, but the tree, now toothpicks, was at fault?"

Lurch said, "Tim seemed to agree to our innocence and also agreed that we probably got one heck of a scare out of this one."

"Good."

"What did Henderson want to know?" Lurch asked. "And will I be next in the line of questioning?"

"I don't think so. Indiana brought up my name in his interview, so I guess Henderson wanted to get a better feel from me about Indiana. Indiana really gets my goat. He hates anyone with any degree of morality, especially me, then uses my name when his name comes into question.

Oh well. But listen to this. When I was setting on the tailgate of Joe's truck to watch Tim's inspection I noticed some interesting things. Number 1. Joe's tailgate was down. Number 2. His tools were a jumble. Number 3. There was mud and I think blood on the end of a spike maul. Oh, and Number 4. Joe has been on vacation for the week. I let Henderson know that the spike maul could be the murder weapon, and he jumped up like his tail was on fire."

Lurch was thoroughly impressed by the news and was getting a charge of renewed energy. I, on the other hand, was sinking fast. We pulled up at the hotel none too soon. I told Lurch that I would see him later and went on up to my room.

CHAPTER EIGHT

SAINT LOUIS, NOV. 12, 1900 EST

started to come to. I slowly became aware that I was in a hotel room, once again. I reached for the TV controls and found a rerun of *Gunsmoke*. I love westerns. The good guys and the bad guys are clearly defined. I was chuckling at Festus when the phone rang: "Railroad calling." I plugged in my numeric information and received the news that I would be on the E156 at 1900 hours with my buddy, Lurch. I showered, packed my grip, and went downstairs to see who I might have dinner with before the trip home. Downstairs I ran into both Indiana and his conductor, Ty. I felt I would rather not partake of nourishment with Indiana, but I wanted to learn why he was throwing my name about and where he was during the time of George's death, so I waved cheerfully at the both of them.

"Hi guys. Are you coming or going?" I asked in my friendliest tone.

Ty waved back. "How are you doing, brother? When do I get to conduct for one of your exciting tree trimming specials, Big Ben?"

"I see good news travels fast. Any time you want a real toothpick you can come with me, Ty. Do you guys want to get a bite to eat?"

Indiana yawned. "Guess so. How about Rondinellis?"

"Sure," I said. "I can drive." Since I shared the cost of keeping an old Honda here at the hotel with three other guys and everyone knew it, I always offered to drive. The two of them said they needed to check in and put their grips in their rooms.

I went around to the back of the hotel to get the Honda and bring it to the front like any good limo driver would. Parking in a spot miraculously available near the door, I wondered how I might pry some information out of the wily Indiana. While waiting, I called Deb to let her know I was safe and ready to start back home after dinner. She acted excited that I had a new story about tree trimming to regale her with upon my return. I had just hung up when Ty and Indiana appeared at the front door of the hotel. They climbed in, and we drove the three miles to Rondinellis. It is a railyard favorite that serves great Italian food and crispy broasted chicken. We were seated in the corner nearest the kitchen. Indiana complained about our seats, not unusual for him.

I said, "Sit down. I only have about an hour to make my train." He reluctantly sat. Ty just rolled his eyes.

While we gave the waitress our orders, Indiana flirted in his usual unseemly manner. I wondered if dinner with him was worth the opportunity to get some information.

As Lurch leaned back in his chair, I told them felt pretty sure everything would be fine after Tim turned in his inspection report and my speed tapes. When I said, "I usually go about five miles under speed, just in case," Ty laughed and said, "Yeah, you do have the reputation of being one of the slowest engineers out there."

"Not like me," Indiana said. "I'm Mr. Fast and Furious." Ty and I just rolled our eyes again.

"By the way," I said, "I had an invitation to speak with Mr. Henderson himself." I sort of hoped Indiana would take it from there. And he did. Indiana dominated the conversation from that point on, both fast and furiously, living up to his reputation.

After listening to his tirade during the meal, I took the guys back to the hotel, hurried and retrieved my grip, and met Lurch in the lobby.

"Hey Big Ben, I looked for you to go to dinner, but you were gone according to the front desk. I walked across the street and had a burger. Who did you dig up to go out for dinner?"

"I ran into Ty and Indiana. We went to Rondinellis for chicken. But my real intention was to gain some information. Indiana was in the mood to give it. I'll let you know the scoop later."

When the limo showed up, it was Betty. "Hi Betty. How's the driving business going?" I asked as I climbed in.

Betty answered between coughs, "Better for me than for some. Do you guys need to stop for food?"

I had leftover chicken, and Lurch said he had purchased a ham sandwich at the diner, so we skipped that stop.

"What did you mean by saying driving is better for you than for some, Betty?" I asked.

"You know the railroad dicks are interviewing Chuck, and his wife is going through chemo again. He's about to lose it and has taken the last couple days off. Why would the police interview Chuck? He was just waiting to pick up a crew. He was right where the bosses told him to be. Doesn't seem fair to me. It could have been me there or any of us drivers. It's just more stress on a man that doesn't need it."

"I agree, Betty. When I get a chance I'll give Chuck a call. Maybe I can alleviate some of his fears. He's a good guy."

"You do that, Ben. See you guys later," she called out in her raspy voice.

We left the van and headed for the office. We were hardly through the door when one of the clerks buttonholed me. I was being summoned to Henderson's office. As I was hustled away, Lurch went on to get our paperwork. Henderson told me to sit, and I did.

He said that he was intrigued by the weird stain, which he thought was blood, and he had asked for the blood and dirt on the spike maul to be tested. He expected some results in a day or two. He asked me again how I discovered it. I went over my actions of the night before. I told him again that I was sleeping on an engine some twenty miles from here on the night of George's demise. Henderson said that had I not had a sound alibi for the night of the murder I would be suspect. Then I asked if he knew that the light over the Mason-Dixon switch and the light over the west end of the yard were out that night. He looked down at his notes, flipped a few pages, and said, "Uh, yes, of course."

I wasn't sure he was telling the truth. I asked if I had permission to leave and board my train. He granted permission, and I left.

Heading out for my train, I noticed Tim at his office door.

"Hey Tim, are my speed tapes okay?" I asked. He replied with an affirmative nod of the head but cautioned with, "No more tree trimming, Ben."

I replied, "Hope not. I like smooth, easy, unexciting trips myself, Tim."

Outside I saw Lurch throwing his grip onto the engine and beginning his walk down the length of the E156. There was no time to loiter. I got busy with my own preparations to leave, and leave we did.

As we settled in for the run, Lurch asked what I had found out from Indiana. I made him wait for our first siding. I thought I could rehash the conversation with Indiana at that point and also put the notes into my phone.

The night was another cold one, but it was clear ansd the moon was at half-mast, the stars numerous and bright, so it was nice to watch the scenery go by even if everything was in shades of gray and black. Late fall, early winter has a solitary feel, like a houseguest getting ready to settle in. I like this time of year. I like crisp nights, emptied fields, shadows, and the expectation of warm fires and apple dumplings.

We traveled some 120 miles before we were ordered to a siding. Lurch and I decided it was time to eat. After finishing my chicken, I took out my phone to enter additional notes. I began by determining the location of the suspects at the time of George's death. I gave Lurch the rundown as I entered these facts into my phone:

Indiana: Earlier during our dinner he admitted that, on the night of George's death, he had been at the casino in St. Louis. The previous night he had gambled away $1600 and was hopping mad, blaming the casino. He had made up his mind to return and win some of the losses back the night George died. That was why he was so furious about getting delayed. He knew he was due some time off by federal mandate, and he didn't want to miss any chance of regaining his losses.

I looked over at Lurch and said, "Indiana was in the St. Louis area the night of George's death. Indiana also indicated that he was certain Henderson didn't have a case without a murder weapon. And Henderson himself cleared the Mason-Dixon. So the ever-prideful Indiana just brushed Henderson off."

Lurch looked over at me, concerned, and mumbled into his ham sandwich.

Next I entered the Mad Russian. MR was being cagey on the subject of his whereabouts. "MR told me that he has been seeing someone down here. They had had an argument so he came back to St. Louis to straighten things out with her. He didn't tell me who she was, but he mentioned that I did know her. Therefore, the Mad Russian was also down here on that night."

Lurch looked over, ready to choke on his sandwich, and declared, "How in the world could both Indiana and the Mad Russian have been back in St. Louis that night?"

I shook my head and continued with my list.

Jesse: She was definitely in the office talking with George.

Chuck: He was waiting out in the lot for a crew call.

Ty: He was in the office talking with Jonesy or more likely complaining with Jonesy.

Jonesy: Was talking to Ty here in the yard office. I need to find out if they were both in each other's company the whole time.

Once I had listed where all the suspects were, I started on the "motivation for the murder" column.

I called out Indiana's name and looked over at Lurch to see if he had any ideas. Lurch chewed on his sandwich thoughtfully before he said, "With Indiana the motive could be almost anything. He complains about child support killing him, but then he goes and loses $1600 gambling. How does he do it?" Lurch's usually low voice started to rise. "His motivation could be anger, finances, or just plain meanness."

I agreed and entered all three motives for Indiana. "Now the Mad Russian, he also has financial burdens trying to keep his kids and going through a divorce. He doesn't like George for keeping him from home terminal any more than the rest of us. I also think that George had pulled him out of service two years back. I need to check on that." I put down finances and revenge for the Mad Russian in the motive column.

Now Jesse. I looked over at Lurch again to see if he had any ideas. Lurch said he knew that George was divorced. On one trip, about a year ago, Lurch had entered Jesse's office to ask a question about a late consist. Lurch saw George give Jesse a swat on the behind, and then he turned to exit her office. George didn't look at all ashamed or embarrassed for inappropriate office behavior, but Jesse looked very embarrassed. "I couldn't tell if she was just embarrassed or furious. It's hard to tell with Jesse," he continued. "Jesse answered my question, and I left the office."

"I agree. It's hard to tell anything about Jesse's moods." I wasn't sure of George's marital status, but Lurch cleared that fact up. I told Lurch that maybe a year ago I had thought there was something going on between the two of them but was not sure. I heard later that Jesse was seeing a conductor out of the St. Louis terminal. I continued, "I don't listen to most of the romance stuff that is discussed over the meals at the hotel. I may try and listen more in the next week." For Jesse I entered as possible motive "romance?"

Now Chuck. I told Lurch that last year George threatened Chuck's position as a limo driver. He was angry that Chuck had stopped for a crew that requested a food stop and then was late for the train. Chuck told me all about it. Luckily, the company said it was acceptable. In fact, they complimented the limo company and encouraged them to instruct their drivers to stop any time a crew requested it. Chuck kept his job. But there was no love lost between George and Chuck due to that incident.

I believe that Chuck had enough pressure at home with his wife and the cancer treatments. I don't think there was enough animosity between the two for a murder. But I wrote down "animosity and finances" as possible motives. Chuck had already declared bankruptcy once. He couldn't afford to lose this job.

I continued by typing in Ty's name. Ty is a relatively new conductor. He hasn't ever been pulled out of service yet. I knew he didn't care for George. Then I noticed a pattern here: no one cared for George. "While I was eating with Ty and Indiana, Ty sat and listened to Indiana's tirade just as I did. I don't know of any possible motive, do you?" I asked Lurch. He said that he knew Ty had a brother and an uncle on the railroad. Lurch suggested that maybe his relatives had had run-ins with George. I wrote down "check out Ty's relatives."

Finally, I typed Jonesy. Jonesy had been pulled out of service twice that I was aware of. George was responsible for one of them. It could be that if he got pulled out of service again, he would be terminated in all capacities. A possible motive for Jonesy could be fear of job loss, revenge, or finances.

Lurch asked why we were not considering others like M&W guys, family, strangers, etc. I answered, "Because more often than not the murderer will be someone who has means, motive, and opportunity. We have just listed possible suspects, alibis, and motives. The means has to involve the spike maul that I discovered in the M&W truck last night. I'm sure of it. And those with the opportunity are those who were at the yard office that night. We will stick with our list unless we find out additional facts that can implicate any others. Just keep your big ears open, Lurch."

We pulled out of the siding, and the rest of the trip went by smoothly. No trees. I walked into the Indianapolis yard, glad that few people were around. I left Lurch to his paperwork and hobbled to my truck. I was still thinking about suspects and opportunity as I drove home. Once home I headed immediately for bed. My wife was sleeping and once again didn't wake. I hit the pillow and slept like the dead.

CHAPTER NINE

INDIANAPOLIS, NOV. 13, WOKE AT 1800 EST

I woke up rather startled to be in my own home and my own bed. I opened the blackout drapes and saw that daylight was waning. It was early evening. I wandered out toward the kitchen and saw my wife reading at the table. She said, "I wondered when you would awake from hibernation."

I replied, "I feel like I have slept through the winter. Every part of me feels ancient. How do bears manage to move all their joints after hibernation? Is my plate in the microwave?"

"Yes. Pot roast tonight with zucchini bread for dessert. You might as well tell me about the trainmaster's death. You haven't been calling me as much, so I know something is preoccupying you."

"Do you feel left out?"

"A bit. But I have been planning for Thanksgiving and Christmas, and working on a project for the college, so keeping busy."

I got my plate and sat down at the table. I told Deb the summary of my notes and asked if she had any ideas concerning "whodunit."

As I gobbled down the pot roast, she asked a few questions.

"Why didn't anyone else notice that the M&W truck's tailgate was down? It couldn't have possibly been down since the murder, too many days passed. Someone must have recently placed the spike maul in the truck. Who was it? Or was someone trying to remove it from the truck? Why couldn't he finish the removal process? Who was in the yard office that night?"

I thought they were all good questions. After thinking and chewing, I jotted down: Lurch, Andre, Tom, and Betty was waiting in the limo. There was another crew I did not recognize. I made a note to find out who they were. Then I made an additional note to find out if the spike maul was being placed in the truck or being removed. I thanked my wife for her good thoughts and plodded to the TV room. She finished up the dishes and came to enjoy the night in my presence, or so I imagined. It was a rare opportunity for us to just sit and watch TV together.

After changing channels several times, we decided we would watch *Magnum PI*. Deb said, "I love Higgins."

"Should I be worried?" I asked.

"Just be glad it's the short guy with a rather wide part in his hair that I love and not the tall, dark Tom Selleck."

"It's us short balding guys that always get our women."

"I think I like his British accent, his ramrod straight stance, and his sense of fair play." As my wife was going into more detail concerning Higgins, my phone rang. I noticed it was a St. Louis area code but didn't recognize the number.

I answered, "Ben Time."

The voice on the other end was somewhat high for a man, but one that I recognized. It was Henderson's.

"Mr. Time, this is Everet Henderson from the St. Louis Railroad Police Department. I have several questions for you. Do you have a minute?"

Yes, Mr. Henderson. I do," I replied as I looked over at my wife and rolled my eyes. I had her attention now.

"Mr. Time"—I noticed we were back to the Mr. stuff—"it is George's blood on the spike maul. It is definitely the murder weapon. The last time the M&W truck was driven was November 5th. Joe Travis, the M&W supervisor, pulled into the east end of the yard and locked the truck at 1700 hours. There is another set of keys in the yardmaster's office for all vehicles left here at the yard. The various yardmasters here don't remember noticing that the keys were missing. Whoever used the maul would need to gain entrance to the truck at least two times. The yardmasters all said they were too busy to notice things like a single set of keys missing. Also, the only prints that we could definitely ID were yours. There were fragments of others, but none we could clearly ID. You have explained how your prints would be there.

"Mr. Time, I have interviewed Joe Travis. He has admitted to knowing you and none of the other interviewees. Question number 1: Why is it only your name he seems to recognize?"

I replied, "I started working on the railroad as a very young man swinging a spike maul, a gandy dancer, for Penn Central Railroad. I have a lot of respect for the M&W department since I was one of them, and I talk with the M&W guys when I get a chance. Other conductors and engineers don't speak often to M&W department employees. In general, transportation employees think they are the top of the pecking order, see, we move the freight. I'm sure Joe recognized Jesse's name as well since he has had to go in and out of the yardmaster's office."

I heard the rustle of papers before Henderson answered, "Yes, Joe said that he did recognize the yardmaster's name as well."

"Question number 2: Mr. Time, when you bumped into the spike maul and looked into the back of the truck, did it seem that the maul had been recently thrown into the bed?"

I thought for a moment before I replied, "I think it was recently thrown back into the truck because Joe is a madman about keeping his tools in order. The tools in the bed were haphazardly thrown this way and that. The maul was positioned with the working end toward my behind and the handle up toward the cab. When properly stored, the ends would have been the opposite direction. Also, it was on top of the other tools. No one would place it that way if there were plenty of time to put it away. It was thrown in with enough force that the handle was toward the cab of the truck and the working end toward the tailgate. I think it was thrown there in a hurry. And either the tailgate was pushed shut without enough force to latch, or there just wasn't enough time for the perpetrator to close the gate. It seems to me that the spike maul was thrown in shortly before I sat down. That's my guess anyway. Any more questions, Mr. Henderson?"

He said, "Not for the moment. Thank you, Mr. Time," and hung up.

Deb was looking intently at me. "Well?"

"That was Henderson. You heard what I told him. Thanks for getting me to think about this just a few minutes ago."

"Does Henderson suspect you?"

"No, I don't think so. After all, I was on my train some twenty miles from the yard while George was getting mauled. Henderson can't get past the fact that I didn't have the opportunity. Joe the M&W guy was familiar with both Jesse and me. However, it really doesn't matter who Joe was familiar with. All the suspects would have known that a spike maul would be in an M&W truck."

"Just be careful, Ben. Mistakes happen in these things, and I have realized through the years as a railroader's wife that there is a lot of animosity between management and union members, and, well, you just never know."

I nodded my head and glued my eyes to the TV once again. We hit the hay about 2200 hours.

CHAPTER TEN

INDIANAPOLIS,
NOV. 14, 1800 EST

T he next morning I awoke and checked to see if Deb was still in bed. She was not. I called my stand number and found that I was three times out. I wandered into the kitchen and saw a note left on the table. Deb was at a ladies' Bible study and would return about noon.

I opened the microwave looking for a hot breakfast, but no such luck. So I made a pot of coffee and put together a bowl of puffed rice, not my favorite, but it was the only box in the cupboard. That meant that diet time was just around the corner. I slathered a piece of toast with a full tablespoon of chunky peanut butter. No diet for me, not this day. I ate, showered, dressed, and looked over my notes about the case. I added that Jesse would have had easy access to the keys of Joe's truck and therefore easy access to the spike maul. If the maul was recently thrown back into the truck, I could only surmise that someone had hidden it for a time and wanted it placed back into the truck just before Joe returned from vacation. If the culprit did know Joe, they would have realized that any tool out of order would alert him. Henderson was looking in the wrong direction. He was looking for someone who knew Joe, maybe someone who knew Joe well. I thought I would look for someone who did not know Joe well or at all.

I heard the garage door go up and knew Deb was returning. She came in cheerfully and chatted about the study. I invited her to lunch, her choice, and she picked the local pizza pub, convenient for a little more shopping. While serving as a pack mule for more Christmas treasures, I got a phone call. It was 1500 hours and Ty's familiar voice informed me that he would be my conductor that night. I could expect my call at 1600 hours. Deb and I decided to get home so I could repack my grip for the next trip. Sure enough, I got the call for work at 1600 hours for duty at 1800 hours for the W367, and Ty was my conductor. I left Deb with a peck on the cheek. She looked up warily. "Why don't you leave the murder investigation to the investigator, Ben? Take better care of yourself."

Ty and I were deadheaded, a limo ride, to Terre Haute to pick up our train. Ty's a pleasant guy, and the conversation was lighthearted. We agreed that the Indianapolis yard had improved recently. They were better about moving the trains into the yard in a timely manner. I told Ty that several years ago it wasn't unusual to get the train all the way to Indianapolis in six hours only to be left waiting just outside the yard for another six. It was terrible to be so close to home and be forced to sit and wait to yard the train. Ty moaned.

"Man, Big Ben. I waited at Cadillac Road for three hours, and that was bad enough. Six hours would be totally unreasonable."

"Well, that isn't all," I said. "We recently lost four new hires who barely had completed all the forms for their personnel folders. They couldn't believe there were no days off, no holidays off, and no weekends off. They just quit."

Ty responded, "I knew about the lack of schedule before I was hired because my uncle and brother work for the railroad. It's not easy, but if you expect the lack of schedule, then at least that's one hump you get over quickly."

I asked where his brother and uncle worked and discovered that both worked out of St. Louis. His uncle was an engineer and his brother a conductor, but his brother was on the list for engineer's school soon, probably in February. Ty said that he ran into them on occasion at the yard office. He added that since most of his family lived in St. Louis, he wanted to eventually have St. Louis as his home terminal as well.

That's one more question I could knock off my list. Ty did indeed have two relatives passing through the same yard in St. Louis, our yard.

Our limo reached the train in Terre Haute. We re-crewed and started toward St. Louis in the night. It was a cold night, and I was glad the engine was warm.

We had not been under way too long when Ty brought up the murder investigation.

"I sure hope Henderson won't be there tonight to grill me some more," Ty whined. The whine was noticeable in an otherwise pleasant man.

"I've been questioned as well, Ty."

"You have? I thought they were questioning only those who were there in the yard office at the time of the murder, Ben."

"I think I was called in to give Henderson insight into Indiana. Indiana walked out on him and mentioned my name during his interrogation. Henderson had the mistaken idea that Indiana and I were good friends. I told him we were work acquaintances. Not friends. Did you know they found the murder weapon? It wasn't the Mason-Dixon but rather a spike maul. That gives Henderson greater authority when questioning now. Make sure if he questions you that you speak the truth, Ty."

"You know me, Ben. I'm your brother from another mother."

Ty got quiet for a time. Called his signals. He stayed quiet until we reached Effingham.

We were cruising. Ty finally spoke. "I didn't like George. He was always trying to show his authority. He was a power monger. He pulled my brother out of service last year. My brother was with an engineer that ran too fast through the yard. They got sixty days out of service for being five miles over speed. My brother warned me about George and told me to stay clear of him. I tried my best. My brother got hurt pretty bad financially from that incident. He has tried ever since to get out-of-service insurance, but the companies won't insure him for at least another year, and only if he remains without further incident. It seems rather unfair since my brother wasn't the engineer. He wasn't the one running the train, Ben."

"I know. They always pull both crew members out of service. It doesn't matter whose fault it is. That is just the way it is, fair or not," I replied.

"My brother didn't think George hated just black men, but all men. The engineer was white."

I nodded, and things got quiet again.

After a few minutes, I broke the silence. "When you and Jonesy were sitting in the crew room the night of George's murder, did either of you hear anything unusual?"

"No, Ben, it was unusually quiet, just the two of us talking. Both George's and Jesse's doors were closed. There was no paperwork to be pulled. It was just quiet. I may have heard the radio, the dispatcher's voice, in Jesse's office. But no other sounds. When I think about it, that was unusual."

"Did either of you leave the presence of the other?"

"Well, I went to the john. At some time, Jonesy went for a cigarette break, and he brought back a cup of coffee. I heard him pouring the stuff into the cup as I was finishing my solitaire game on my phone. Wait a minute, while he was pouring his coffee I heard a door open or close, because I thought after hearing the door that we would be soon on our way. That didn't prove to be the case."

"How long was Jonesy gone, and about what time did he come back? What time was it that you heard the door?"

"I think Jonesy was gone about fifteen or twenty minutes. I'm not sure. I was playing Spider Solitaire on my phone, as I said. It was about 0330, Ben. You don't think Jonesy or I did it, do you?"

"No, but Henderson will be asking more questions, maybe these questions. I'm certain of it."

We quieted once again. I thought as I watched ahead in the black of the country night that I would have several more facts for my notes when this trip was done. Ty did have a motive. George hurt his brother financially. Ty and Jonesy were not in each other's presence the whole time that night. At least fifteen or twenty minutes were unaccounted for. I also had several more questions pop into my mind: Why were both office doors closed? Where were both Jesse and George? Was there some dispatching going on that could verify or refute Jesse's alibi? Was the door sound one of opening or closing? Which door was being opened and why? Why do I always end up with more questions than facts? I ruminated on these problems as we were given permission to enter the St. Louis yard.

I brought the train to a halt, a perfect four-horse stop I thought to myself. Ty jumped down with his grip, and I followed somewhat more slowly. Ty was several sets of tracks ahead of me when he turned around and yelled "Ben!" and pointed behind me.

I turned around just in time to see a coal hopper headed right for me. I moved as fast as I could, and I barely avoided becoming another railroad accident statistic. As I stepped over the rail, I turned in time to step up on the ladder of the coal hopper, climbed to the platform, and set the hand break, bringing the stray car to a halt. I hadn't performed this move since I was a yard conductor in Burns Harbor many years before. I climbed down, and Ty came running back. He huffed out, "Didn't know you had it in you, Ben."

"I didn't either. Where did that car come from, Ty?"

"I don't know, Ben. I turned around and there it was. Let's look around. This gives me the chills."

We walked back the way we came, looking for any movement, man or beast. There were two trains on the track with the stray car. Both trains were heading west. The car must have been from the rear of the last train. I guessed it could have been improperly tied down, but still wasn't sure. We didn't see anyone around.

"Let's go into the yard office and explore this further," I suggested.

Ty agreed. Then he said, "Do you think we should report this? You know they will try to blame us somehow, and your heroic gesture to stop the car will be considered an illegal move, Ben. You will be in hot water."

"Maybe I will just explore for a while and then decide whether to report the incident."

We entered the yard office. As Ty walked toward the computer to finish up the paperwork, Henderson appeared and said he would like a word with him. I walked toward the trainmaster's office. He was speaking with Indiana. I nodded and asked where was Indiana's conductor. I only wanted to find out both who and where his conductor was. Indiana said that the Mad Russian was probably getting the paperwork or taking a smoke break. I had passed by the computer and knew that the only one getting paperwork was Ty, so I continued out the front drive entrance to the yard. Chuck was sitting there in the parked limo. He rolled down the window and asked if we were ready to board. I said, "Not yet, Chuck. Ty has to speak with Henderson."

Chuck rolled his eyes at the mention of Henderson's name.

As I got closer, I asked if he had seen the Mad Russian.

"Well, I brought him here, Ben," said Chuck.

"Yes, but have you seen him come out on a smoke break?"

"No. I haven't seen him since he was delivered here."

I thanked Chuck and told him we would see him soon. I turned and walked around the building looking for the Mad Russian or anyone else who may have purposely sent a coal hopper my way, but I didn't see a soul. Back at the office, as I entered, I saw Jesse sitting in her chair, head down, looking over paperwork.

"Hi Jesse, how have you been? Haven't seen you around lately. Must be working opposite shifts."

"I don't have much time, Ben. We have two trains that have to get out soon and only one crew here. Ya, we must be working opposite shifts. Talk later."

"Are we short yard conductors too?" I asked.

"Of course. I have two coming in. We haven't finished making up the second train yet," she said as she answered the phone.

I didn't ask who the last yard conductor was. If this was just a mistake, and the car was improperly tied down, I didn't want the conductor in trouble. It seemed my near demise was either due to someone who didn't tie down the car properly or someone like the Mad Russian, Jesse, Indiana, or even Chuck trying to scare me or terminate me. I hated thinking that. I thought it would be in my best interest not to report this incident. Instead, I should try to figure it out. I saw that Ty was coming out of Henderson's office. I asked Mr. Henderson if I could speak with him a moment.

He nodded and waved me toward the door. "Mr. Time, I was just going to ask you the same thing."

I entered and took a seat. Henderson remained standing and said that he had interrogated both Indiana and the Mad Russian again. "I won't divulge what they have said, but I am considering having the trainmaster pull them both out of service. Can you enlighten me as to why that would be an unwise decision?" he added.

"Well, I guess I would need to know why you are considering pulling them out of service."

"Indiana now admits he was in the area the night of the murder. He had threatened George. He's been employed by the railroad thirty-nine years, so I am sure he would know that an M&W truck contains a spike maul. He would also probably know where extra keys are kept. He had means, motive, and opportunity

"The Mad Russian is lying to me, Mr. Time, but I'm not sure why. I don't know if it is to protect himself or Indiana. I'm not sure if I want Indiana behind bars or just out of service for now, or if I want the pair free to hang themselves."

I thought a moment and looked straight into Henderson's beady eyes. "Mr. Henderson, you seem to have made up your mind that Indiana is guilty, but you still seem suspicious of the Mad Russian. You only have circumstantial evidence against Indiana. Let me ask you, was Indiana here in the office the night or the day before I found the spike maul?"

Henderson looked down at his notes. "Indiana was not embarking from this office or debarking that day or evening."

"Then I don't think it was him. Someone threw that maul in the back of the truck a short time before I found it. I'm sure if the tailgate were down several days, someone here would have noticed, so it had to have been thrown in just prior to my sitting there."

"Not necessarily. Several crew members may have passed by and paid no attention."

"That could be true, but a yardmaster or trainmaster would have noticed if the tailgate were down for several days. Have you questioned them on that point?"

"No I have not, but I will."

Still looking Mr. Henderson in the eyes, I said, "I think you only have circumstantial evidence and should keep collecting facts until you have real evidence. It is unwise to pull the pair out of service before all the facts are in."

Mr. Henderson frowned, but then he informed me that I was dismissed. He stopped standing and sat down.

As I took my leave he was paging through his notebook. I headed for the limo. Ty was already in the back seat, so I threw my grip in beside him and took the navigator's seat beside Chuck.

"Hi Chuck. How are you and your good-looking wife doing?" I asked.

"Hey Ben. We're doing a bit better. Her chemo is still making her sick this time around. I took a couple of days off to be with her. In addition, I was getting a bit upset being interviewed by this Henderson fellow. You know, Ben, I can't afford to lose this job right now. I was just sitting here the night of George's death waiting to pick up my crew and nothing more. How in the world can they suspect me?"

"Chuck, they have to interview everyone who was here that night. It doesn't mean they were targeting you. Hey, they even interviewed me, just because I know Indiana. Don't worry. This will all blow over soon."

"Ben, there was no love lost between George the Tyrant and me. Last year he tried to get me fired because a crew was late for their train, and I had stopped so they could pick up a meal for the trip. Luckily the limo company stuck up for me and said that was part of my job description, or I would have lost the job. I really didn't like the man, but I never would have killed him. I heard it wasn't a switch but a spike maul that killed him. Is that true?"

"It's true," I said as we arrived at the hotel. Ty got out of the van and handed me my grip. I saluted Chuck goodbye and we entered the hotel. Steve was at the front desk handing out cookies. I signed in, took my cookie, and told Ty to get some beauty sleep.

Once in my room I sat down in the sun-faded chair that had been set too close to the window. I began to think through the past hour. Was someone trying to do away with me? It wasn't long before I nodded off.

CHAPTER ELEVEN

SAINT LOUIS, NOV. 15, WOKE AT 1600 EST

awoke with a charley horse. I jumped up to put weight on the offending calf. I hopped around for a minute or two. Then I walked up and down the length of the bed like a normal human biped. Thinking that this was no good way to re-enter the land of the living, I sat down on the edge of the bed and messaged my left calf muscle. I pulled the drapes and saw that the sky was laden with clouds. I wasn't sure if they were snow clouds or rain clouds, but some precipitation was definitely on the way. I showered, dressed, made a cup of coffee, and ate my cookie.

Since I was once again in the land of the living, ready to think about the yard incident, I sat down at the small hotel room desk and wrote out some notes on the thin tablet. Beginning under the hotel name, I listed the names of those who could have uncoupled the train car. Jesse, Indiana, Mad Russian, and Chuck. I guessed reasons that each one might want me in heaven immediately. Someone on my list may think I saw something the night of George's demise. I noticed that Henderson said he was aware that Indiana was in St. Louis that night, but he didn't mention that the Mad Russian was also here that night. That made me think the Mad Russian had not confessed the truth that he too was here. I knew the truth. Maybe MR wanted to cut me down for that reason. I had a hard time believing any of them would seriously try to get rid of me. But the stray car seemed to be a tightly targeted threat. My suspicions were leaning toward the Mad Russian. First, because I never did locate him at the yard office, and second, because I was the only one who knew the truth of his whereabouts on the night of the murder. Could it be that the Mad Russian was indeed the killer? I needed to find out if he had passed through the yard office the day or night I found the spike maul.

I was yanked away from these thoughts as Ty called and asked if I would drive over to the Applewood restaurant for dinner. I said sure, and we took off for restaurant style home-cooked nourishment.

As we were enjoying our meatloaf dinners, Ty leaned over the table.

"Ben, do you think that stray car was a plan or an accident? I think about it a lot."

"Ty, I just don't feel that sure about it. It really keeps me puzzled. Did you see the Mad Russian anywhere last night?

"Not me, Ben. I never saw him at all."

"Okay, Ty. Let's just keep it between us, okay? I don't want to get some poor fellow in trouble just because of a little bad luck. It's hard enough when you don't get blindsided."

"I understand, Ben. I'd hate to get some poor guy in trouble over something out of his control."

We topped off our meal with a great piece of homemade apple pie. The pie is the big draw for the Applewood restaurant. It draws railroaders like flies.

When we reached the hotel, I told Ty that I needed to go back to my room and give my wife a call. As he headed for his own room, he said he was going to get in touch with his brother.

Back in my room, I called my stand number and found out we were four times out. That surprised me. It looked like I might get "held away" pay. That is pay for each hour over fifteen hours held in the hotel. The board has been turning so fast for the last three months I haven't made any "held away."

I would much rather be held at the home terminal than in the hotel. I called Deb to let her know that I was fine, but I was four times out and probably wouldn't be home for two more nights. I would keep her abreast of my homecoming just in case she needed to get her boyfriend out of the house. I kept the conversation light and full of my one-liners. I didn't tell her about the runaway train car. After our conversation, I lay on the bed and watched

The Virginian. At the end of the second episode I was surprisingly tired enough, once again, to sleep.

The next morning I awoke at 0700 hours, a normal daytime hour to wake. I showered and went downstairs for breakfast. As I entered the dining room I looked around to see if I might join any of my fellow trainmen for breakfast. I saw Jonesy drinking his coffee, but he hadn't got his food yet.

"Hi Jonesy, would you like some company?" I asked.

"Take a load off, Big Ben, and I do mean a load," he replied.

"That one's getting old, Jonesy," I said as I looked up at the waitress, who had just arrived.

"Hi Ben. Have you had enough time to look over the menu to order?" she asked.

"Haven't looked at it, but don't need to. I'll take two eggs over easy, two pieces of wheat toast, and two slices of bacon cooked crisp."

She poured me some coffee and topped off Jonesy.

"Did you just get here, Jonesy?"

"We pulled in about an hour ago. It was a good run, so I'm not quite tired enough to hit the hay. Thought I'd get breakfast first."

I sort of liked saying, "I'm on 'held away.' Can you believe it? First time in three months! Maybe the work is slowing down some. I wish it would. I'd like to spend a little more time at home so near the holidays."

"Me too, Ben. Have you heard anything more about the murder?"

"They found the murder weapon, a spike maul, or rather I found it. Long story. It has to do with my tree trimming incident."

"Oh yah, I know about that. Good job, Paul Bunyan."

"Has Henderson been interviewing you every time you come through the office, Jonesy?"

"This was the first trip that he hasn't called me in. I hope that's a good sign. I told him all I know, even told him that I didn't care for George the Tyrant. George set me up for a failure, Ben. He was hiding in the bushes and got me. I was out of service ninety days for that, and that was my second incident. Next one will mean I will be pulled out of service in all capacities. Fired."

I noticed Jonesy's voice got louder and louder as his sentence progressed toward the word "fired." Several people at nearby tables were staring.

"Jonesy, quiet down some," I said as I looked around the room. He caught himself. I saw him swallow hard, and then he settled down.

"See, Ben, I don't like George. He was conniving and power hungry, but I didn't kill the guy."

"Bear with me for a minute as I ask you some questions about the murder. I think Henderson is looking at the wrong man as the murderer. Where were you the night of the murder when you went for a smoke break?"

"I went out the yard door, smoked two, came in, and went out the drive door, thinking that I might text my daughter before we got on our train."

"Did you see Chuck in the limo?"

"Yeah. I did. He looked as if he were asleep. I finished up my text and went back in. I poured some coffee before I returned to the crew room to complain to Ty."

"What time was that?"

"I think about 0330 hours, but not sure. I was just getting anxious. Ready to be on my way home."

"Did you see or hear anything unusual that evening?"

"Can't say that I did, Ben. You know, you sound just like Henderson."

"One last question. Check your time book. Were you passing through this yard either November 11th or 12th before 0400?"

Jonesy looked at his time book. "Hmm. I was leaving Saint Louis on November 11th at 0600."

"That's the end of my questions."

"Ben, you don't suspect me, do you? I'm just beginning to feel a letup on stress from Henderson. Who do you think Henderson is targeting?"

"I think he's targeting Indiana. And as much as we don't care for one another, I don't think Indiana did it. I don't want to think anyone has done this. But once Henderson sees the flaws in his thinking, he may come back around to you, Jonesy. I would like to get this whole

CHAPTER ELEVEN · 97

thing solved, the murderer brought to justice, and the rest of us out of the limelight and back to normal."

"I guess I had better get back to my room and get some sleep. You're bringing me down, Ben. The stress of being a suspect is returning again. Thanks a lot. See ya."

As Jonesy walked away, shoulders humped and head down, I felt a little sorry for him. But I did notice from his answered questions that even though he was here when the spike maul was thrown into the back of the truck, he was at the yard too late to have done it. And he was not there when the rail car came too close to my backside.

I was finishing my third cup of coffee when I heard my phone go off. It was Ty. He said, "Ben, I just got a call from Jake the Horse Setter. You know him. He is another new hire. He said that they arrested Indiana. Indiana is being brought back here to jail, here in St. Louis. They think Indiana did it, Ben. Indiana was in the yard when your near miss occurred too. Do you think he was responsible for that?"

"I'm not sure he is responsible for anything, Ty. I'm going back to my room to think. Thanks. Talk later, Ty."

I climbed the stairs to my room. Not for exercise, but it was a good time to think. I looked over my notes, and I just couldn't put Indiana here to throw the spike maul back into the truck. Indiana was definitely a hothead, and he seemed to hate me and my values, but I didn't think he did the murder or set the car free to get me. I sat on the chair for a while. Then I lay down to watch *Magnum PI*. I noticed that Magnum was often trying to help those who were not his best friends. In fact, it was often his worst enemies. When the episode was over, I called my stand number. I was two times out so I decided to call the local jail and see if it would be possible for me to visit Indiana. The female voice said Indiana had just been led to his cell. I would have to go through proper security steps to visit.

I got the old Honda started and drove to the St. Louis jail. They gave me some strict orders, and I followed them. They led me to a room where I could visit Indiana by phone. I could see him, but I could not touch him behind the bulletproof glass. Indiana looked horrible. He hadn't slept in about twenty hours. He sat and looked back at me through the transparent partition.

I put the phone to my ear. "Hi Indiana, you look pretty tired."

I could see him nod weakly before he spoke. "I'm sure surprised to see you, Ben. It's good of you to come."

"I'm two times out right now. I'm getting some 'held away' for the first time in months. I have the time."

He looked me straight in the eye and said, "Ben, I didn't kill George. I may have wanted to, but I'm no killer."

"Did Henderson tell you why he thought that you were George's murderer?"

"I told Henderson that I came back here and went to the boat to win back money that night. I guess he got some video from the casino that verifies I was there, but it verified I was there from 2200 hours until 0200 hours. That video apparently left me time enough to commit murder and return to Indianapolis, according to Henderson. Why are you here, Ben?"

"Because as you told me earlier we are union brothers, Indiana. And I don't believe you are the murderer."

At that Indiana began to tear up. He looked at me and just mumbled out, "Thanks."

"Would you mind if I pray with you right now? With you, and for you?"

Saying this took a bit of courage on my part since Indiana had made it very plain on many occasions that my faith was not welcome in his presence. He nodded. I bowed my head and prayed for him, for courage and peace and for his release.

"Dear Lord, you are a very big God. One who knows the number of hairs on our heads. One who keeps our tears in a bottle. That means you care so very deeply for our sufferings. Thank you, Father, for your great love. I bring to your throne room today my brother, Indiana. You know him, Lord, and his dilemma. Please, Father, give him patient endurance like you gave your servant Paul. Please, Father, give him hope and peace, and allow the truth of this murder to be found out so my brother will find himself released. Thank you, Lord, for this brother in need and your great care. Amen."

When I finished and opened my eyes, his head was still bowed. He slowly raised his eyes and said, "I'm sorry for all the degrading remarks that I've made about you. I have at least on several occasions attended Sunday school, a long time ago, with a cousin whose mother felt sorry for me. My father was a drunkard and beat my mom daily, along with me and my brothers and sisters. I left home as soon as I could. I lied about my age and started working for the railroad when I was only seventeen. The one thing I haven't done is beat any of my ex-wives or kids, Ben. But I sure haven't been what I should have been for any of them. I'm not a beater. I'm not a killer. I have a lot to think about now and plenty of time to do so. Thanks, Ben, for coming."

I asked if he had access to a Bible, and he nodded. "Read Psalm 119 if you get the chance, Indiana. Don't be afraid to look in the table of contents to find the book." Indiana nodded again. Then he rose and walked through the door behind him.

After he disappeared, I got up and departed through my own door, still praying silently for the man that had made my life and so many other trainmen's lives miserable.

I received my work call on the drive back to the hotel. I had just enough time to grab a sandwich and get ready.

CHAPTER TWELVE

SAINT LOUIS,
NOV. 17, 1400 EST

We boarded the train. All went smoothly. Once in Indianapolis, we put the horses away. This was the kind of trip I liked most—unremarkable. It was approaching midnight, so I didn't call Deb to warn her of my imminent return. At home I raided the refrigerator and turned on the TV. I wasn't tired enough to lie down. I found a rerun of *The Virginian* and, as my wife says, "zoned out." I woke myself snoring with my skull doing the bobble head thing. I guessed it was time for bed. The next morning, I woke to the smell of sausage cooking, coffee brewing, and my wife humming in the kitchen. I love home.

"Breakfast is almost ready. Give me five more minutes."

"You must have missed me," I replied as I took my seat at the table.

"I did, and if you are going to be home for a while, we are going to have lunch with the kids today."

"That means it must be a weekend."

"It is. It's Saturday—all day today."

I sometimes forget the day of the week. Nights and days just go by, without anything remarkable to separate one from another. Deb placed the hot breakfast plates on the table and two steaming cups of coffee. She said grace, and I dug in. She popped up and brought two napkins back to the table.

"How was your time in St. Louis? Anything new on the murder case?"

"They have arrested Indiana, but I don't think he did it. I had a good visit with him yesterday in jail."

"You went to jail to visit him?" she asked rather surprised, because she knew Indiana and I were not fast friends.

"I did, and I prayed with the man. I think we understand each other better, and I have great hopes for his spiritual growth."

"Great!" she said as she popped up again, this time for salt and pepper. "Who do you think did this?"

"Give me some time and I will let you know. Now where are we meeting the kids, meaning my youngest daughter and her husband?"

"We're running to the bank, the post office, and a store at Metropolis. Then we meet at the corner restaurant there."

"That means I need to shower, dress, and put on my running shoes. Right?"

"Yep, but what a hearty breakfast you have had to start off your day!" she said as she cleared the table.

I went off to the shower knowing the good breakfast was part of a feminine plan, but I was happy to be duped.

We set off for the morning. It was Saturday, the 18th of November, at 10:00 in the AM. I have to remind myself every so often of day, date, and time just to be part of the real world, or rather the non-railroad world. After my wife informed me that we needed some cash from the ATM, I drove through and retrieved some of my actual cash that I work for. I was almost stunned into silence, since I see it so infrequently. We then went to the post office. I made the mistake of offering to go in for the stamps. Deb said great, because she was going to give our daughter a ring.

I walked in, and I was shocked to see the line winding back through to the first entrance. I checked my watch. I had to ask myself, why is everyone at the post office on this Saturday, the 18th of November, at 10:35? I stood looking toward the three clerks wondering why the line was so long. Each clerk was busy, no one was lollygagging. One clerk was dealing with mail, probably for a business, by the looks of the customer's large plastic carrier. Another was weighing and stamping a number of boxes, and the final clerk left his station to walk away for some reason. I checked my watch again. Five minutes had passed without the line moving one inch. At this rate, I would still be in line when the post office closed.

I thought about the near miss with the car in the yard the other night. I hadn't reported it, but when it was discovered by one of the yard conductors, things would certainly back up for a while in the yard, somewhat like this line where I was currently standing. It would make the yardmaster's life miserable, and paperwork would mount because of the incident. I couldn't see Jesse, the yardmaster, turning the car loose. It would just make her own life miserable. I thought I could take her off the list of suspects for this incident. That brought me back to the Mad Russian as chief suspect, or I could try to tell myself that the whole thing was simply an accident. I definitely needed to talk to MR.

Twenty minutes after I entered the post office, I was able to leave with two books of stamps. I had a good speech ready to let Deb know exactly why the post office was in the red. However, I found she was still on the phone with our daughter. The unhurried passage of time was not disturbing her.

I turned the radio on as I started toward the Metropolis outdoor mall and found some happy oldies. I began singing along with the Beach Boys, and Deb finally finished the conversation with a person she was going to see in just an hour, our daughter.

"What store are we headed for?" I asked.

"I need to find something for the Thanksgiving table, you know to make it more . . . Thanksgiving like."

"Okay, better question. Where should I park?"

"Park on the southeast corner of the mall."

Now we are getting somewhere, I thought, as I drove around the mall two times to find the parking place. I guess everyone wasn't at the post office as I previously thought. A good portion of the population was here. We went to a store that women love and men follow closely behind, ready with a "That's nice," hoping to get out with little time and expense invested. I performed my part with the "That's nice," but it didn't save me either time or money. *Oh well*, I thought, *you win some and you lose some.*

We met the kids at the Irish restaurant. I was ready for some man talk with my favorite son-in-law.

The hostess set us in a secluded corner. At last we could hear one another speak. My daughter and wife began by showing each other their newly purchased items. My son-in-law ordered an Irish lager. I ordered ice tea. We all chatted as we ate the crisp Irish fish and chips. My daughter and son-in-law were both employed in the medical profession, and they had a lot to say about a wave of layoffs due to the implementation of Obamacare. They were worried about how this big change might affect their lives.

"It is scary not knowing if you will have a job the next day," said my daughter. Her husband nodded. "We don't know whether to be relieved we're still working, or not. Every day somebody else gets the axe." We listened to their very legitimate worries and tried to reassure them.

"I know what you mean," I said, silently praying I would know the right thing to say. "We have survived many layoffs, and we have both changed professions. We count on God's help when things worry us." We know that they know we are always praying for them, but today it seemed important to be sure they knew.

After a nice meal and great conversation, they went their way to finish some errands, and we went ours. Deb needed to stop at one more store in the mall. Then she took my arm and said, "You up for a movie?"

I really wanted to say yes, but I thought about the way things had been going.

"I'd love it," I said, "but I don't think it would leave me time for any rest before the next call." It irks me that they seem not to mind scheduling my calls so close together.

It was hard to turn her down, but she laid her head on my shoulder and said, "You're right. Let's get you home."

Once home I plunked down in front of the TV hoping to catch a *Gunsmoke* rerun. I was in luck and found one playing on one of the uppermost channels. Deb sat down and worked on a grocery list for Thanksgiving and her Christmas gift list. Miss Kitty was once again trying to protect Matt with some well-placed innuendos in her saloon to help catch the bad guys, who were seeking revenge for capture of one of their own. We both jumped when my phone rang.

I saw that it was Lurch so I picked up.

"Hey big guy, how's it going?" I asked.

"Not bad, Ben. Have you heard about Indiana's arrest?"

"I have. I even had a chance to speak with him," I responded.

"Do you think he did it, Ben?"

"No I don't. Indiana couldn't have thrown the spike maul back in the M&W truck before I discovered it. He said he didn't do it, and I believed him." As I was speaking I realized that Lurch didn't know about my near miss with the coal hopper.

After I related the details of the incident, he asked, "Ben, do you think that the incident was on purpose?"

"I really don't know but I am going to have a good long talk with the Mad Russian. He may be my conductor tonight. I hope so."

"Okay. You be careful." Lurch sounded concerned.

Gunsmoke had ended, and I knew that I better try to get some rest before the call. I gave Deb a kiss, and off to my pad I hobbled. I was about to doze off when I thought, *Hey, I think I get it.* But as I tried to put the thought together, it evaporated and I fell asleep.

CHAPTER THIRTEEN

INDIANAPOLIS, NOV. 18, 2300 EST

The call came at 2100 hours for 2300 hours. I asked the dispatcher who my conductor was for this trip. Just as I had thought, it would be the Mad Russian. I got up immediately to shower and pack and be mentally alert for the trip. My wife was surprised that I hadn't slept for an hour as usual after the call. I hadn't told her about the escapee car incident, so I didn't let her in on my reason for being in alert mode. She wouldn't understand that I was preparing to question the Russian. She had packed me a lunch, and uncharacteristically she stayed up until I left the house at 2230 hours.

Once I reached the railyard, I looked for the Mad Russian's truck. He was there on time. In the office, I spotted him at the computer getting the paperwork. I said, "Hey," and walked back to my locker.

In the locker room, several of the guys were discussing Indiana's arrest. Most were gloating. I pulled on my boots and left for our assigned train. Concentrating on the required preparation procedures, I really wasn't aware of the Mad Russian's presence until we were ready to leave. We left the yard as prescribed with very little chitchat. I would pick the time and place to question him. After we went through Terre Haute things would quiet down with few radio calls, signals, or other distractions. That would be a good time to bring up some of my questions. Soon we were on the west side of Terre Haute. The night was cold. There was also the possibility of snow showers that night, but we hadn't seen any. About the time we arrived in Casey, Illinois, our engine was warm, the radio was quiet, and talking would help keep the Mad Russian awake. I asked him what he thought about Indiana's arrest.

"I'm glad they caught him," said the Russian, fidgeting a little in his chair, "and I'm glad I won't have to travel with him. Maybe things can get back to normal."

"You know, Russian, Indiana admitted he was in St. Louis the night of George's death. Did you admit you were there as well?" I knew he had not, but I wondered if the man would be truthful with me.

He was quiet for a moment. "I didn't need to tell Henderson. My personal life is none of his business, and I knew that I hadn't committed the murder."

I thought about that statement for a bit before continuing. "Indiana is in jail because he did admit he was in St. Louis gambling. They had video from the casino to prove it. He admitted to the truth. You did not. I don't believe he did it."

"So you think I am worse than Indiana because I didn't tell my whereabouts?" The Russian's voice began to rise ever so slightly. "Worse than a man that did nothing but put others down and especially put you down, Ben. He hated you, and you know it."

"I know. However, I don't think he committed murder."

"Well, I didn't commit murder either." The Mad Russian stood as he made this declaration, as if he had somewhere to go.

I kept my eyes on the track ahead while the Russian belatedly remembered that he was captive in the engine and sat down again. I decided to keep quiet for a time and let him stew. We were quiet all the way to Effingham. I was radioed to move to the siding, not unusual for this run. Things would soon be quiet again. After I pulled off to allow the van train to pass, I looked over at my comrade, and he was pretending to sleep. I knew he was pretending because his eyelids were moving in conjunction with his thoughts. I opened my lunch and decided to make some noise chewing on my apple first. My wife was trying to get me to eat healthy. After several good crunches, the Russian shouted out, "Could you eat something less noisy? I'm trying to sleep!"

Just for meanness, I took another bite as loud as possible. Now that the Russian was conscious again, I began questioning again. "You know, Russian, the other night in the St. Louis yard I was crossing the tracks toward the office. A wandering coal hopper barely missed my behind. I managed a few old moves from my conductor days and brought the car to a standstill. I understand you were at the yard office then, and I just wondered if you knew anything about the incident?"

The Russian looked straight ahead. He was silent a long time. I was patient a long time.

He finally replied, "That was my fault, Ben. The yardmaster was giving me a hard time. I was sick of her. I knew that if a car was found on the lead, it would really mess up her night. I didn't mean for a near miss. You are always at least ten to fifteen minutes behind your conductor when you dismount. I saw Ty and figured I had the time to release the car. I had no idea you were right behind him. I'm sorry, Ben. I will never pull a trick like that again. I'm sorry. See, I do tell the truth if it matters. I pulled a dumb trick, lost my temper. I will never do it again."

"When I could not find you, I thought that you were involved," I replied. "You could have killed me, Russian, just to screw up the yardmaster's night."

"I'm sorry, Ben," the Russian said as he stared straight ahead in the night.

I stared at the starless sky. A few snow flurries hit the windshield as we progressed toward St. Louis. I needed some silence to mull over this new information.

Other than calling signals the rest of the trip was quiet. I watched the sunrise over the sparse clouds. The light was diffused and gradually shifted from orange to yellow. The scene had a way of giving hope.

Once I entered the yard office I thought again about what the Russian had said. It was true. I usually am fifteen minutes behind my conductor. I saw the Russian walk by Jesse and completely ignore her. She gave him the look of death as he passed by. I wondered what the relationship between the two of them really was.

It wasn't unusual for there to be bad blood between trainmen and management. Most trainmen, if wise, kept their distance from female managers because there had been so many sexual harassment accusations within the company. I decided that, on the return trip, I would poke about the Russian's mind to get an idea concerning his relationship with Jesse and what it might have been with George.

I was pretty beat by the time we got our limo for the hotel. I made it up to the room, disrobed, and immediately fell asleep. I awoke and looked at the clock. It was 9:00, or 2100 hours. I fell asleep around noon in the light of day and awoke in the dark of night. I felt as if I had slept for a thousand years. I thought I had better call my stand number. The automated reply was that I was two times out. I wasn't quite sure if I should try and sleep some more or get up and get some food. After a few minutes, I decided to go for nourishment. There was a Denny's nearby that was open twenty-four hours. I thought that would do. I showered and took the elevator to the hotel lobby. The door opened, and blocking the entrance—or should I say filling the entire opening—was none other than my pal, Lurch. I thought I would try his line and greeted him with "Good evening," drawing out the "eve-ning."

He said, "Hey Big Ben, what a surprise to see you here."

"Funny, Lurch. Have you eaten? I'm going over to Denny's. Do you want to come along?"

"Yeah, sure. Let me get this grip up to the room. I'll be back down in a few."

We exchanged places in the elevator, and I walked over to speak with Steve at the night desk while I waited for Lurch.

"How's it going, Steve?"

"Not bad, Ben. Things have been unusually calm here. I hope it stays that way and this is not the calm before the storm. Even the railroaders have been peaceful. Do you think it's because Indiana is locked up?"

"Could be. I have heard much less in the way of the usual complaints from the guys." I grabbed a cookie from the warmer. The cookies are one of the best amenities at this hotel. I decided against a cup of coffee just in case I had time enough to get a little sleep on a siding. As I was enjoying the cookie the elevator door opened and Lurch's huge frame exited. He certainly could be scary at night.

"Ready to go, Ben."

I nodded and finished munching on the warm, luscious treat. We walked out the doors and headed across the street to Denny's.

The hostess was a familiar face. "Haven't seen you two in a while," she said as she gathered up menus. "Do you want a booth or table tonight?"

"A booth." We followed her to the far side of the room, noticing the place was nearly empty.

"Is business slowing, or is it just slow now?" I asked.

"It is just slow now. Not late enough yet for the late-night crowd."

After the waitress took our order, we began to talk in earnest. Lurch drew circles on the tabletop with his finger.

"I heard Indiana is still in the pen. He couldn't get anyone to bail him out. The guy's life is so messed up, Ben."

"I know, but he is on my prayer list now. And besides that, I do believe he is innocent."

"I know you do. Have you learned anything from the Mad Russian concerning the near miss?"

"That's what I wanted to talk to you about. The Mad Russian admitted to me that he released the brakes on the car. He said he wanted to really mess up the night for Jesse. He claimed he didn't want to kill me or anybody. MR added that he thought I would be fifteen minutes behind my conductor as usual. He even apologized for the near miss."

"That's some dangerous stunt, Ben. He could lose his job."

"I have to think about that one. Two things bother me. One, he didn't speak the truth about his whereabouts the night of George's demise. He really thinks it is okay to lie when it suits him. Two, he took the chance of endangering others—me, or somebody else—just to get back at Jesse. I thought I knew him better. I had thought well of him for trying to keep his kids from his wife when she was on drugs. I guess I never knew him that well at all. If the Russian was angry with Jesse and released the car in the yard, what might he do to George if he were angry with him? I also think the Russian was here in the yard in the timeframe that would have allowed for him to throw the spike maul back into the M&W truck. MR isn't the least bit sorry that Indiana was arrested for George's death."

"So you think the Mad Russian did it, Ben?"

Just then the waitress returned with our food. I watched as she placed the hot breakfasts down in front of us. We thanked her and occupied ourselves with our food until she had left.

"It's beginning to look as if the Mad Russian is the most likely suspect. I want to find out more about his relationships with both Jesse and George on my return trip."

As Lurch placed a gob of jelly on his toast, he cautioned, "Take care, Ben."

We both needed to think about the Russian and ate our breakfasts in quiet thought. Finally, Lurch broke the silence. "Did you ever find out who the Russian's new girlfriend here was?"

"When he first confessed to being in St. Louis, he said he wouldn't tell me her identity because I would have known her. He still hasn't told me."

"Ben, this may be way off, but could his girl be Jesse?"

I crunched on a slice of bacon and rolled this through my gray matter. I hadn't thought too much about his girlfriend, but what if it were Jesse? I glanced up at Lurch's huge forehead with admiration and said, "You know, Lurch, your big head may be worth more than a big hatrack. I will be thinking on this some more tonight."

Lurch smiled and drank down his orange juice. We finished our food, left a good tip, and crossed back toward our hotel. Lurch said he was looking forward to sleep and once again cautioned me to be careful on the train trip home. I thought I needed some sleep, but when I got back to my room, I slumped into the only comfortable chair. My mind was in a whirl.

If indeed the Russian's girlfriend was Jesse, that fact would place him in the yard office the night of the murder. He lied to Henderson concerning his whereabouts. For some reason, he released the brakes on the coal hopper, a very dangerous move. He was in the yard at the proper time to throw the maul in the truck. The more I thought about the facts, the more the Russian looked like a murderer. I didn't like thinking this one bit, but the facts! I couldn't avoid it. After an hour or so I thought I should call Henderson and tell him what I knew.

It was late when I dialed Henderson, but surely he was used to railroad hours.

Henderson answered, "Mr. Time, I haven't heard from you in a few days. I thought our conversations would be over now."

This man sure didn't know the meaning of gracious. I answered with, "Mr. Henderson, I'm sorry to call so late, but I have some information about George's murder that may interest you."

"I have that case all sealed up, Mr. Time."

"Well, you still don't have a timeframe that Indiana could have returned the spike maul. I have some additional facts concerning my conductor, the Mad Russian. He was Indiana's conductor when Indiana threatened George. Perhaps if you interrogated him again in my presence you could obtain some new facts that are pertinent to this case. Interrogating Jesse as well may shed some light on the case."

"Why do you need to be present in the interrogation?"

"I think you are more likely to get the truth if I am present."

"When will you and your conductor be in the yard office?"

"I'm now one time out. Probably when they call the E133 train."

"Do you know if Jesse is working tonight?"

"You can call and check."

"I will. See you tonight, Mr. Time. This better prove worth my time."

He hung up. I hoped I was doing the right thing. If I was correct, the right man would be put behind bars. If I was incorrect then I would have lost a friend. I was much too edgy to relax and go to sleep.

CHAPTER FOURTEEN

SAINT LOUIS, NOV. 20, 0100 EST

received the work call at 2300 for 0100. I was still awake thinking about how the upcoming interrogation would go. Even though all evidence pointed toward the Mad Russian, I had the nagging feeling that there were some facts still missing. I attributed the uneasy feeling in my gut to my initial fondness for the Russian. He had his share of problems at home. His wife had become addicted to drugs and was an unfit parent. He did all he could to help her and try to keep the family together. His effort wasn't enough, and then he had his hands full keeping his kids. He only managed with the help of his mother. Somehow the picture of a faithful husband, dedicated father, and dutiful son did not fit with the picture of a liar and malicious avenger who murders or even risks murdering someone.

119

I grabbed my grip and started toward the hotel lobby, my mind working on overdrive. When I reached the lobby, I saw that the limo was there with the Russian waiting in the front seat. I threw my grip in the back seat and greeted Betty and the Russian with a brief "Good morning."

Betty's gravelly voice was even deeper at this hour of the morning.

She replied, "Do you need any food for the trip, Ben?"

I really wasn't interested in food; must be the worry and the fact that I had several packs of peanut butter crackers in my grip, so I answered, "No, not this trip."

Both the Russian and Betty turned around and looked at me with the "I don't believe it" look.

"I got crackers," I said. "Trying to lose weight before the holidays," I added.

They both laughed, and off to the yard we went.

The Russian beat me out of the limo and headed immediately for the yard office door. I told Betty goodnight, hefted my grip, and followed MR to the yard office. As I entered, I saw Henderson sitting in the extra office with Jesse and the Russian already seated. Henderson wasted no time. He motioned me in as well.

The Russian immediately started complaining. "Why am I here again? I thought this thing was over."

MR looked straight at Henderson. He didn't glance at Jesse or me. I looked over at Jesse and noted that she was watching the Russian—not Henderson, not me. Her brow was furrowed, and there was a fierce look in her eyes. "Why are we here?" she asked.

Henderson didn't seem the least bit moved by their anger and said, "I need to clear up a few things."

He began with questions addressed to the Russian. I was pretty sure they were the same questions asked of him the first round. Most of the questions were about the day that Indiana threatened George. Then Henderson turned to Jesse and asked her why George had not assigned the first train to leave the yard, my train, to Indiana and the Russian.

Jesse responded, "I don't know. That's not my concern. I don't assign trains. I just want them out of the yard."

Henderson continued, "Wouldn't it make more sense to have assigned Indiana and the Russian to Ben's train because they would have had more time to work and not exceed federal regulations?"

"As I told you, assigning trains is not my job.'"

Henderson addressed Jesse again. "Did George ever mention to you that he had a problem with Indiana?"

Jesse looked down and responded, "No."

"Did George ever mention having a problem with the Russian here?"

Jesse looked straight at Henderson and said, "George didn't discuss his feelings toward trainmen with me." This time her voice raised in intensity and pitch. The Russian turned and stared at her, and if looks could kill, she would have been laid out. As Henderson stared at her, his small eyes somehow became even smaller.

Something about her answer made me question the assumption that George was trying to make Indiana's life miserable. Perhaps George was trying to make the Russian's life miserable instead.

Henderson questioned the Russian again. When He asked, "Where were you the night of the murder?" I looked straight at the Russian. He glanced at me and looked down. I wondered whether he would tell the truth this time. He seemed to go into a temporary coma. Henderson waited. I waited. Jesse squirmed in her seat uncomfortably. Then he said, "Here, in the yard office."

Henderson jerked his heard up, and this time his eyes were as big as saucers. I must have been staring a hole into the Russian. Jesse dropped her pen. That got my attention, and I looked over at her. Her fingers were shaking as she picked it up.

Henderson said, "You know that statement contradicts your initial statement, Mr. Stravinsky." Henderson glanced at me as he said this.

The Russian stared at the floor and nodded.

Henderson looked over at Jesse and asked, "Did you see Mr. Stravinsky in this office the night of the murder?"

Jesse appeared to be quite flustered and stammered, "I don't know, the trainmen come and go, one night is the same as another here, and I'm concerned with the trains, not the crews."

"Are you telling me that the night George was murdered seemed the same as any other night, Ms. Rikes?"

She didn't respond, and Henderson looked over at the Russian. "Why were you here at the yard office, Mr. Stravinsky?"

"Listen, Henderson. I am telling the truth now. I was here to speak with Jesse. We were seeing each other for a long time. We had an argument, a misunderstanding. I wanted to clear things up. I was here for one hour, and then I left for home. George was alive and well when I left. I heard him yelling into the phone. I didn't want to be suspected, because I didn't need the hassle, and I did not kill George."

Henderson scribbled something on his tablet. Then he looked up and asked, "Will you two gentlemen please sit in the locker room while I speak with Ms. Rikes alone, and under no circumstances leave this yard office." We exited his office.

I went and grabbed a cup of coffee while the Russian went to the locker room. I heard the clear sound of a locker getting pummeled so I decided to remain out next to the computers for the time being.

I started thinking about the possibility that George was getting even with the Russian that night and not Indiana. I think we all assumed George was getting back at Indiana because Indiana is such a loudmouth. But if George was jealous of the Russian and Jesse, he could have kept Indiana and the Russian here in St. Louis longer just to be nasty. It came to me that Lurch mentioned the possibility of something between George and Jesse, because he, Lurch, had observed George being rather too familiar with Jesse one night by hitting her on the behind

What if the Russian was jealous of George and came back to put an end to his rival?

I wished I could hear the questions being fired at Jesse. I stepped one step closer toward that office door. I could only hear a male voice. I could not distinguish the words. I decided to stay away from the Russian for the moment and stood there between the computers and the office door sipping my coffee. It seemed there was now even more evidence against the Russian.

The Russian's lying to Henderson made me first suspect him, but I knew by this time that Jesse lied as well in her initial interrogation. She didn't admit that MR was here that night. Maybe it was because she was involved and cared for him, but maybe there was some other reason. Something went wrong with their relationship or the Russian would not have set the coal hopper loose. Jesse could have killed George because she was here that night. She had the keys to the M&W truck and could have replaced the spike maul before I found its working end in my behind. I hadn't thought that much about her because I, along with most trainmen, have the preconception that management sticks together and union workers stick together—just another wrong assumption.

I could now number my misconceptions. Number one: a management employee would never get angry with another management employee. I have seen considerable evidence to the contrary. A management employee could indeed want another management employee fired or dead. Misconception number two: a woman would not commit murder. Again, there is considerable evidence throughout history to the contrary. Misconception number three: a woman wouldn't have the strength to heft up a spike maul. Most women on the railroad have to be able to lift fifty pounds. A spike maul weighs less.

I realized that I had too many misconceptions, too many prejudices in my thinking. Jesse had means and opportunity. I was unsure of motive, but it could be there as well. She stayed away from work for several days after the murder. We just thought that as a woman she may have been fond of George and needed some time to grieve. This may not have been the case. . . Maybe just an additional misconception.

I needed to ask the Russian some questions about Jesse while I had the chance. I walked into the locker room bolstered with courage to face the Russian.

I sat down across from him. He said, "Do you think better of me now, Ben? I told the truth about where I was. Now, what if Henderson thinks I did it and comes after me? I have to be there for my kids, Ben." He put his face in his hands.

"Russian, do you know if George and Jesse had anything going on between them?"

He looked up slowly from his hands and said, "Yes, Jesse said that they saw each other for a short while, but she decided to call it quits. George wasn't very happy and tried some of his power tricks on her, the same way he treated everybody else."

"When you came back to the yard office the night of the murder, did Jesse seem upset?"

"She sure was. I thought it was because I accused her of being overly friendly with all the guys, George included. I think George held Indiana and me out away from home because he was jealous of me and Jesse, not because he was mad at Indiana. But then he was always mad at Indiana as well, so it's hard to say."

"Why were you mad enough at Jesse to put your job on the line and my life on the line the night you set the car loose?"

"Jesse became very distant. She wouldn't take my phone calls, treated me like dirt. Even after they locked up Indiana for the murder, she still wouldn't speak with me. At first maybe she thought I did it, but later even after Indiana was looked up, well, I just don't understand women. The night I set the car free, she told me to get out of her life or she would file a sexual harassment claim against me. I just lost my temper, Ben. I told you I was sorry."

"Have you noticed any inconsistencies in her overall personality, Russian?"

The Russian was standing now, energized with his testimony, and answered, "She seems to be able to flirt, love, hate, and shut people out on a dime. Almost the same as my ex-wife acted on drugs, now that I think about it.

I don't know, Ben. Maybe I just bring out the worst in women. Or am I just a bad judge of them? I don't know. . ."

"Last question, Russian. Did you murder George?"

"I can't believe you have to ask, Ben. Of course not. I didn't like the guy, but I did not murder him."

The Russian walked out of the locker room. I guess he needed a break. I looked up my original notes about the case on my phone. I now had an idea who the murderer was.

I rose and walked to the office door where Jesse was still being interrogated and knocked. Henderson yelled, "Come back later!" I persisted and knocked again. I heard his chair slide across the floor. He opened the door and said angrily, "Didn't you hear me, Ben? Come back later."

I replied, "Mr. Henderson, I know who killed George. May the Russian and I come in?"

He opened the door wider and gave me a scathing look. I turned and asked the Russian, who was standing by the computer, to follow me in. He did so with his head down. We both took our seats. I asked Mr. Henderson if I might ask a few questions, and he nodded in the affirmative. Jesse just sat there acting quite perturbed that we were wasting her time. Henderson picked up his pen and said, "You may proceed, Mr. Time."

I glanced down at my phone notes and asked, "Who is responsible for the lighting in this yard?"

Jesse responded, "I am."

I continued, this time addressing Mr. Henderson, "Have you recorded that any lights were out in the yard on the night of George's murder?"

He paged through his notes for several minutes. The rest of us were silent. Finally, Henderson stopped paging and said, "There were two lights out in the yard. One was directly over the Mason- Dixon switch and the other over the west end of the yard."

I turned toward Jesse. "Why were the lights out? There should have been an order signed by you to have M&W change them, correct?"

She looked me straight in the eyes and said that they had probably just gone out, and in all the commotion she hadn't had the chance to have them replaced.

"What are the chances that two lights would go out simultaneously?"

"I don't know, but apparently that can happen. They were both out."

"Do you know how long the lights burn before they need replacing?"

"I don't know. What's this all about, Ben?"

"I believe all lights that are replaced are recorded because of cost and maintenance orders that are processed, so the burn life could be checked, is that correct?"

"Yes, it could be determined. So what?"

"If we look at past records, then we could determine if both were replaced at the same time when they previously burned out. We could figure out how long they had been out before it came to your attention by looking up past records."

I turned back to Jesse.

"Did you tell Henderson that the night of the murder you and George were talking as the W123 passed through the yard? And that George thought the crew of that train was in violation so he left to check the switch?"

Henderson started paging through his notes again, and Jesse nodded. Then I addressed both Jesse and Henderson. "Do either of you know the crew members who were on that train?"

Jesse just looked at the floor. Henderson paged through his notes. In a few seconds he named the crew members as Frank Mercer, engineer, and James Best, conductor.

I looked directly at Jesse and asked her if she knew either of these men.

"Of course I recognize their names. I recognize the names of most trainmen that pass through this yard."

I asked her, "Do you know at least one of these men better? Have you had or are you having a relationship with one of these men?"

She stood and shouted, "None of your business or anyone else's who I see!"

Henderson said that he could subpoena her to answer, and he could call each of the two men in for questioning.

Jesse sank into her chair. When she spoke, she could barely get the words out

"I have been seeing Frank Mercer."

The Russian's head jerked up, and he stared a hole through her.

At that moment, I was very sure I could piece together what happened the night of George's murder

When George said that he was going out to the switch to pull that particular crew out of service, Jesse followed. She had the keys to Joe's truck and retrieved the maul under dimly light conditions. She walked up behind the switch that George had moved back into position to set up the crew for a failure and whopped him one. She wiped some of the blood from the spike maul onto the switch armature. Then she put the maul in her car. She may have planned to put it back into the truck but got nervous and feared some interruption, so she put the maul in her car. She returned to her office and reported the incident as a switch accident. When Lurch and I got to the yard office, I remember seeing Jesse pass by, and she was going toward the front door, toward the parking lot. Until tonight I could not think of a single reason that she would be headed that way in all the confusion. I now think she was concerned that there may be some evidence, dirt, blood, etc., that could be spotted on or in her car, so she went back to check it over.

Jesse interrupted and said, "You have no proof of anything you are saying, Ben."

"I think there might be proof, Jesse. I think that once you had the spike maul home you did not clean it thoroughly but instead just flung it in and out of the ground several times, leaving it a dirty mess, and then threw it back into Joe's truck. You must have been in a rush the night you threw it in as well. Henderson took blood and dirt samples off the maul. I bet we can match the samples to some in your vehicle."

Jesse stood quite suddenly, surprising us all. She shouted, "I hated George, I really hated George. He was a tyrant! He came on to me just a week after I started working here. I was lonely, left my husband, and came here not knowing a soul. I thought our relationship was fun for a while. George got his kicks out of harassing and setting up trainmen for failures. He also got his kicks out of controlling me. I tried to end the relationship over and over. He threatened my job, and he threatened anyone I tried to have a relationship with. He set up engineers and conductors to be pulled out of service, or he harassed them by holding them here away from their home terminal. Ask the Russian. George was harassing him that day because he was jealous. It was not Indiana like everyone thought. George didn't like the fact I was seeing the Russian. He was setting up Frank and James to be pulled out of service because I had just started seeing Frank. He didn't care how this affected anyone financially, mentally, or at all. He didn't care. So when he went out to the switch, I hated him. I hit him hard with the maul."

Jesse appeared completely calm as she continued, "I think when the lights went out in the yard, about two days apart, Ben, for your information, I just let them go and didn't file a maintenance order. I must have started thinking of the plan then. The plan just started to materialize the week before like a fog being burnt off a plain to make this look like a switch accident. It almost worked didn't it, Ben? Didn't it, Mr. Henderson? When Joe turned in his keys and was going on vacation that week, I decided that would be the perfect time. I still wasn't sure I could do it until George went out that night to set up the crew. He just opened the door and laughed as he went outside.

"I lost it. I went to my office, put on my gloves, grabbed the keys to the M&W truck. I got the spike maul out of the back of the truck, walked up behind George, and let him have it, right in the temple as he turned to see me. It was surprisingly easy, and I was glad, happy even, that he saw me right before the blow. I wiped some blood from the spike maul with a handkerchief and wiped it onto the switch stand lever ball. I saw a shadow in the yard office, so instead of putting the maul back into the truck I hurried to my car and dropped it into the trunk. I then went back around the east end and entered the yard office. I reported the switch accident.

"During the confusion that followed, I got to thinking that maybe I had gotten some blood on my bumper, so I went back out to check. You were right, Ben, I was going back out to my car. When I got home that day I just put the whole thing out of my mind. The next day I called off work and took the maul out of my car while it was parked in my garage. I took it out in the backyard at night.

It didn't look too bad. I wiped it once and dug in the ground in my flowerbed. It needed some weeding anyway. I thought that would clean the maul enough since I didn't think it would ever be found out as the murder weapon. I guess I was wrong on that point. I also cleaned my trunk carpet with Resolve. You may find fiber matches for blood and dirt, or you may not. I no longer care. I am confessing because I did the company, myself, and the trainmen a favor getting rid of George. Maybe you can make me a deal for this confession. How about it, Mr. Henderson?"

Mr. Henderson was busy writing and recording the confession. He paused for a moment, looked up at Jesse, then asked her to continue.

Jesse continued with her confession, seemingly wanting to get all the details out in the open. She said that when she had returned to work two days later she then thought she had better return the maul to the M&W truck before Joe returned from vacation. She left the yard office unobserved, opened the tailgate of the truck, and heard some footsteps. It was Tim, the trainmaster, coming out to greet and inspect our train that had turned the oak into matchsticks. Jesse admitted that she just threw the maul into the truck bed and headed out of sight.

I returned my attention to Jesse as she continued, "I'm glad I did it. George was an abuser and dictator. The trainmen should applaud me."

Jesse then looked at the Russian and said, "Sorry, Russian. You came along with too much baggage, kids, ex-wife a drug addict, just too much baggage."

The Russian kept his eyes on the floor.

Henderson stood and said, "Mr. Time, you and your conductor can proceed and take your train home."

The Russian and I closed the door softly behind us. I had been completely surprised by the confession. I was having some trouble preparing myself to become Big Ben, the engineer. The Mad Russian was going about his preparations for the return trip like a robot. Luckily, I didn't have much to do with the paperwork. I just needed to get to the limo and be shuttled to our train. I walked out the door and made my way to the waiting limo. It was Chuck. He seemed to be his chipper self as he greeted me, "Hey Ben." I got into the back seat and greeted him and told him the Russian would be out shortly. The Russian followed and got into the front seat. Chuck revved the engine, and we were off for home.

Our trip home that night was silent with exception of signal calling. The Russian didn't doze off, and I couldn't doze off. At times I thought about Jesse and her confession, and at times I zoned out just unable to fathom a murderess. I had never heard a real murder confession before. I sure didn't think she would confess so calmly, almost taking pride in her deed. It appeared that she thought she had done us all a favor. It was all so troubling. I wondered as our trip progressed what the Russian was thinking.

We arrived in the Indianapolis yard without incident. I took my grip and went home ready for sleep. I hit the hay and slept like a log. When I woke, it was dark about 6:00 or 1800 hours. I made my way to the kitchen where my wife was finishing up some dishes. I asked, "Did I miss my supper?"

She replied, "Your plate is in the microwave. I would have waited to eat if I had known what time you would wake."

"That's okay. I'm just glad to be home," I said. I took my plate of baked chicken, broccoli, and a baked potato from the microwave and sat it on the kitchen table. "I guess we are serious about trying to keep our weight in check this holiday season, aren't we?" I asked as I began to shovel the meal into my mouth.

"Yes, we are. I am not going to gain the usual eight pounds over the holiday this year. We just have to try and eat right, Ben." She had finished the last of the dishes and sat down across the table from me with a glass of water.

"How did this trip go, Ben? You seemed in a hurry to get out of here when you left the other night."

It was time to tell my tale of the last couple of days. I finished up with Jesse's confession.

She looked over at me and said, "Well, I am glad it wasn't the Russian who did this, or any other of the trainmen that I've heard so much about. I guess I shouldn't put it that way. I am very sorry it happened at all. How do you feel, Ben?"

I scraped my plate clean, took it over to the sink and rinsed it, and placed it in the dishwasher. It was hard to put my finger on it.

"I'm not really sure how I feel. Maybe a shower will help me sort out my thoughts."

"That sounds good. Go for it. I'm headed upstairs to type the first draft of our Christmas letter."

"Isn't it too soon? It isn't even Thanksgiving yet!" I said.

"No, I need a first draft now. You know me. I need to be ahead of the deadline. I can refine and add more after Thanksgiving."

She headed upstairs, and I went for the shower. I made it a long one. When my daughters were home, I would have yelled at them for such a long shower. They used to deplete the hot water tank. I planned to do the same.

Once dressed I went to the TV and found a rerun of *Gunsmoke*. I watched without a single thought passing through my mind until my cell rang. It was Lurch. He had just made it in from his trip.

He wanted to know what was going on. He had heard in St. Louis that Jesse was arrested for George's murder. I went through the details of her confession. I had to thank him for recognizing that the Russian's girl could have been Jesse. I was still trying to figure out how I felt about the way things had worked out. It helped to go through the developments that night. As I told him that at first that clue pointed to the Russian being the murderer, it reminded me how easy it had been to jump to conclusions. It felt good to think through the way Henderson's interview turned up the fact that Jesse, too, had means, motive, and opportunity. I didn't previously suspect her because I had a lot of misconceptions and prejudices, and I listed them off to Lurch. Lurch seemed relieved it wasn't the Russian as well. Like me, he found it hard to believe Jesse was in fact a murderer. He added that it was truly difficult to really know a person.

"Ben, you may be surprised, but I did take your advice and talk over my schedule with Kim. I brought up the possibility of living together too. You will probably be glad to hear that we decided to give our dating relationship some time to see how she handles the schedule or lack thereof. She seemed relieved that I was willing to take more time. I think we both feel better about the decision to give our relationship the opportunity to grow before we try to settle major decisions like marriage. I wasn't too happy with your advice several weeks ago, but I feel different about things now. Thanks, Ben."

"That's great, Lurch. I wish you both a God-blessed relationship."

I have always appreciated Lurch as a fellow trainman, but after this conversation I felt sure our friendship would have a deeper dimension in the future. I looked back at the television and noticed that *Gunsmoke* was over. *The Rifleman* was on. My mood now elevated, I sat down to enjoy the show. My cell rang again. I was tempted not to answer, but it was Indiana. I would be missing a good show, but I decided I should take the call.

"Hello," I answered.

Indiana yelled into the phone. "Big Ben, did you hear? Jesse has been arrested for George's murder. See Ben, I told you I didn't do it. I told the truth, Ben. I didn't do it."

I replied, "I'm glad to hear it, Indiana." Reluctant to mention my involvement, I said, "I guess you're out of jail."

"I was released two days ago. My third wife came up with the bail money. I think she wanted me back to work for the child support. I can return to work tonight. I will probably get the W145 for 0100. I never thought I would be so happy to go to work, but I am. One last thing, Ben. Thanks for visiting me in the clink. I needed someone to believe me, and you did. I won't forget it, Ben. Thanks."

And just like that, he hung up.

I was still enjoying the afterglow of Indiana's happy call when Deb came down the stairs.

"Ben," she said, "remember how we always start the Christmas letter with a Scripture verse? I was wondering if you like Psalm 119:160 for this year. It says, 'All your words are true; all your righteous laws are eternal.'"

"How did you come to think of that one?" I asked.

"Oh, it's been on my mind for a while. The women's Bible study has been studying Psalm 119, and that verse just took root in my heart. I've been thinking about it all week."

"Wow, Deb. Did you hear my phone ring? That was Indiana on the phone just now. He's out, he's back to work, and he called to thank me for visiting him. When I was there with him in the jail, I remember suggesting he read Psalm 119 for help. I think God picked this Scripture for us. It would be perfect for this year's Christmas letter."

I gave her a hug, feeling some much-needed peace and joy. God had acted in the midst of all our misconceptions to show his eternal truth and righteousness.

ABOUT THE AUTHOR

T. A. Huggins was born and raised in Northwest Pennsylvania. She received her PhD in Leadership Administration in Higher Education from Indiana State University. She taught Anatomy and Physiology for the majority of her teaching years. This is her first fiction work. She has published some fifty-plus Christian articles for various denominations. She is married to a retired locomotive engineer and has two adult daughters. They live in Avon, Indiana, during the summer and fall and live in the Tampa Bay area in the winter and spring.

Morgan James
Speakers Group

www.TheMorganJamesSpeakersGroup.com

We connect Morgan James published
authors with live and online events
and audiences who will benefit
from their expertise.